If This
Is Home

If This Is Home

Kristine Scarrow

DUNDURN
TORONTO

Editor: Shannon Whibbs
Copy editor: Alison Kooistra
Design: Jennifer Gallinger
Cover design: Laura Boyle
Cover image: Composite image by Laura Boyle. Girl on swing © Antonio Guillem, Rye © ortodoxfoto.
Printer: Webcom

Library and Archives Canada Cataloguing in Publication

Scarrow, Kristine, author
        If this is home / Kristine Scarrow.

Issued in print and electronic formats.
ISBN 978-1-4597-3650-4 (paperback).--ISBN 978-1-4597-3651-1 (pdf).--
ISBN 978-1-4597-3652-8 (epub)

        I. Title.

PS8637.C27I32 2017   jC813'.6   C2016-903879-3
                                                  C2016-903880-7

1 2 3 4 5   21 20 19 18 17

Conseil des Arts du Canada   Canada Council for the Arts   Canada   ONTARIO ARTS COUNCIL CONSEIL DES ARTS DE L'ONTARIO an Ontario government agency un organisme du gouvernement de l'Ontario

We acknowledge the support of the Canada Council for the Arts and the Ontario Arts Council for our publishing program. We also acknowledge the financial support of the Government of Ontario, through the Ontario Book Publishing Tax Credit and the Ontario Media Development Corporation, and the Government of Canada.

Care has been taken to trace the ownership of copyright material used in this book. The author and the publisher welcome any information enabling them to rectify any references or credits in subsequent editions.

— J. Kirk Howard, President

VISIT US AT

dundurn.com | @dundurnpress | dundurnpress | dundurnpress

Dundurn
3 Church Street, Suite 500
Toronto, Ontario, Canada
M5E 1M2

*To Ben. If home is where the heart is,
then my home is where you are.*

Chapter 1

"Jayce, can you feed your sister for me before you go?" my mom calls from her bed. She's lying down again instead of going to work. She's been missing a lot of work lately. I sigh and drop my backpack to the floor. I was just about to leave for school, and if I don't get out of here soon, I'll end up being late. Again.

"Can I have some Corn Pops?" my little sister, Joelle, asks. She's giving me her sad puppy-dog face.

"No. We don't have any," I tell her.

"Toast with jam?"

"No, we're out of bread."

"Eggs?" she replies hopefully.

I glance into the fridge and survey its contents. Ketchup, mustard, butter, cheese slices, a jug of Kool-Aid, a bruised apple, and a half a head of lettuce that has turned colour and is sitting in a pool of brown liquid. There is also a litre of milk that I take out and shake to feel how full it is, but there are only a few sips left.

I open the cupboard door, hoping to find food that I know wasn't there yesterday, but all I see are the same items. Soda crackers, a few cans of chicken noodle soup, and spaghetti noodles. The thought of having spaghetti again is almost too much for me. It's pretty much all we've been eating for weeks now. With butter and salt and pepper, or with melted cheese slices on top, or mixed with ketchup. I am sick to death of spaghetti noodles. As much as I know Joelle dislikes them, I spot a bag of rolled oats. A perfect breakfast.

"Yuck. I hate that stuff," Joelle says when she sees the bag of oats.

"Oatmeal is good for you," I tell her. "Besides, it keeps you fuller longer. That's a good thing."

Having something to keep our bellies fuller longer is a good thing right now, because lately Mom's paycheques haven't been enough to keep us afloat. Her jobs at the supermarket and the diner never paid much, but Mom's take-home pay is even less now that she has been missing so many shifts.

"You gotta put sugar and milk in it," Joelle pouts.

"Yes, Ellie," I reply, calling her by her nickname. "I will."

I pour some water into the bowl of oats and pop it into the microwave for a minute and a half. When I pull the bowl out, it is hot. The mixture is thick and steamy, and I sprinkle some sugar on it from the can on the kitchen counter.

"Just a little bit of milk, okay, Ellie? We have to make it last."

"It looks like puke," Joelle says, staring down at the lump of oatmeal in front of her.

"It looks perfectly fine," I say sternly.

"I can't eat this," she says, finally, pushing the bowl away.

"Joelle Marie, you *will* eat it!"

"I want something else. Please, can I have something else?" Joelle pouts, tears forming in her eyes. I'm so frustrated that she won't eat. What does she think this place is? A restaurant? And why can't she just eat what's put in front of her? Doesn't she know that there is nothing else?

Of course, she doesn't. Mom has always been able to provide for us; it's only in the last few months that we've struggled to get food on the table. At first Mom tried to shield us from the reality of our situation, pretending that everything was fine. She'd bring home leftovers from the diner and play it off like we were getting a real treat — which they would have been, if they were hot and fresh. Soggy french fries, dried-out garlic toast, and limp salads only felt like a treat the first time around.

Ellie doesn't need to know the truth. So I am doing the same thing as Mom, pretending that everything is okay, that we're like any other family.

"How about some crackers?" I offer.

"Okay," Ellie agrees.

I pull out a handful of crackers from the plastic sleeve and hand them to her. I pour the remainder of the milk into a cup, but there's only about an inch of milk left. I hate the fact that I have nothing else to give her. Now I know how Mom feels.

Ellie hums to herself happily and bites into the crackers. I spoon the oatmeal into my mouth, not wanting to waste anything. It's thick and pasty, but the sugar gives it enough flavour.

It's only the third week of May. That means there is still a week left before Mom's next payday. This won't be enough food until then. We have a few days' worth, tops.

"Ellie has had breakfast," I say to my mom. I peek my head through her bedroom door. Mom's long, thin figure is barely visible through the blankets, except for the fan of blond hair splayed across the pillow. She's always had long, gorgeous hair that hangs in natural loose curls. I wasn't as lucky. I was blessed with straight, mousy-brown hair that has no style at all.

"Thanks, J.J.," Mom whispers. She doesn't even move or look up at me.

"Whatever," I mutter. "Don't forget about lunch for her." I've been feeling a lot like the parent these days.

I've always been the one to take care of Joelle at night while Mom works. She's often had more than one job to keep us afloat, and so she's had to work long hours. She usually works five days a week at the supermarket from eight o'clock until five o'clock, and then four nights a week at the neighbourhood diner from six o'clock until eleven o'clock. Even when mom is working every shift, though, we seem to barely have enough to keep a roof over our heads. By the time rent is covered, food is bought, and utilities are paid, we usually live like kings for the first half of the month, but run out of food and then coast on whatever is left for the last couple of weeks until Mom gets paid again.

Joelle is only four, so she stays with our elderly neighbour, Mrs. Johnson, until I get home from school. Mom doesn't have to pay her very much, which is a good thing, because we don't have the money for a regular daycare. Mrs. Johnson doesn't do much with Joelle — she spends most of the day watching soap operas. But Joelle is pretty quiet and good at playing by herself. She invents little games and imaginary friends. She really is no trouble.

In fact, Joelle wins over everyone's heart. She's heart-stoppingly beautiful. She has hair like my mother — long, blond, and naturally curly — coupled with bright blue eyes and long, thick eyelashes. She could be a pageant princess or something, the way everyone always gushes about what a pretty child she is. Even though we are sisters, there is little resemblance between us, aside from us both being thin. She is the spitting image of my mother, while I look more like our dad.

Since Mom is staying home again today, Joelle will be staying home, too. She likes being home with Mom, even though chances are Mom will be spending most of the day in bed.

"Bye, Ellie," I say, kissing her on the top of her head. "Be good. Let Mom rest."

"Bye, J.J.," Joelle says back. She's bitten her crackers into the shapes of what must be animals, and she's playing out a scene with two of the shapes while chewing on the cracker bits in her mouth.

I look at the clock. I've got to get to school. I've been late far too often lately. My first period teacher, Mr. Letts, has been less than impressed with how many lates I've gotten this term. I grab my backpack and head out the back door, knowing that if I run down the back alley, I can shave off a bit of time getting to school. It's a brisk morning, and I'm thankful I decided to throw on a jacket today. The side streets are pretty quiet, but then, they always are. We live in one of the oldest neighbourhoods in the city. There are a lot of elderly people who live here, and a mix of different cultures. The houses all tend to be on the smaller side and many of them sit in various states of disrepair.

I gather speed as I approach the first of two busy streets I need to cross before getting to my high school. There's a break in traffic, and if I run for it, I can make it across the street without having to wait for the light to change. A car seems to speed up as I dash across the road, honking as it zooms past. I feel the rush of the wind from the car as it lifts my hair. Reaching the other end of the road, I step onto the sidewalk and catch my breath. My heart is pounding, and I can feel beads of sweat on my forehead. Suddenly I'm far too warm for this jacket. I peel it off, stuff it in my backpack, and start running again.

"Jayce, you're late again!" my best friend, Amanda, whispers to me as she passes me in the hallway. She's walking with a teacher, and they are both carrying stacks of textbooks.

"I know, I know ..." I whisper back, hoping that the teacher doesn't hear me.

"Don't forget, we're going out for lunch today," she reminds me.

Amanda just got a car, so we've been leaving the school grounds every chance we get. The only thing within walking distance of our school is a convenience store, so being able to drive to get lunch somewhere is a big thing. Amanda's parents gave her a car when she turned sixteen. It's not new or anything, but it's still pretty awesome.

I'm still in driver training, not that it really matters. The only car we own is a 1980 Ford station wagon that's been parked like an oversized lawn ornament in our backyard for as long as I can remember. My mom doesn't drive. We take the bus for everything.

I grab my binder from my locker and slam the door shut. I'm hoping I can somehow still sneak into class before Mr. Letts notices, but the last bell must've rung quite a while ago, because the hallways are deserted. I'll probably get detention today, which means that I won't be able to head out with Amanda and our other friends. Then I realize that detention would probably be a blessing, anyhow. I don't have any money on me, and the thought of sitting in McDonald's or Wendy's watching everyone else eat would pretty much be mental torture.

"Miss Loewen," Mr. Letts acknowledges me as I enter the room. Isn't this guy ever late? Why are teachers always so on time? Sure enough, everyone is sitting in their desks and the lesson has already started. I duck my head down and rush to my seat, my cheeks burning with embarrassment.

"You'll be spending some time in detention again, I see," he says. He stares at me for what feels like forever, just to prolong my embarrassment.

"Yes, sir," I respond, flipping open my binder. There are some giggles from around the room, but I ignore them. Mr. Letts takes the cap off a dry-erase marker and starts writing on the board.

"As we discussed before, we have an important day coming up," he says. He turns toward the class so that we can read what he has written:

TAKE YOUR SON OR DAUGHTER TO WORK DAY

Some of the students cheer.

"Sweet! One day out of school!" someone says.

"Woohoo! The stereo shop, here I come!" says another.

"I get to be a cop," the girl beside me says.

"What if your parents are on welfare?" a boy yells out. Most of the kids laugh at this, but our high school is hardly filled with students who are well off. It's situated in one of the poorest neighbourhoods in the city. Although he's trying to be funny, *somebody* here must be on welfare.

What if your mom doesn't go to work anymore? I want to ask. *And you don't have a dad who lives here?*

"You can always go to work with another relative, as well. An aunt, an uncle, a grandparent — even a neighbour. Next Monday is the big day. I want these sheets filled out after you're done. You can hand them in on

Tuesday. I want to know all about your experience. What did you enjoy? What was the most challenging part? Do you think you'll follow in your parent's footsteps?" Mr. Letts starts handing out the sheets. "Remember, these need to be signed by your parent and the company supervisor where they work."

I want to laugh. I can go work a shift at the supermarket or at the diner. Hardly great career material. Why couldn't she have a better job? Why couldn't she be something cool like a vet or a nurse or something? A feeling of guilt creeps over me. I know my mom has worked long hours over the years. Her jobs may not be glamorous, but they've gotten us by, and Mom's a really hard worker. *Or was,* I think. You need to actually go to work to be considered a hard worker, and Mom doesn't do that anymore. Maybe she's just burnt out. Years of working double shifts must have taken all the energy out of her. *But what if she doesn't get it back? What then?*

I tuck the handouts from Mr. Letts into my binder and listen to the chatter around me. Most of the other students seem really excited about this assignment.

My dad isn't around. He's a musician, a guitar player, in a band called Raven's Spell. I've never seen his band play, but my mom says that years ago they were really going places. If things were different and my dad was in my life it would've been cool to go to a gig with him or something. Everyone would be jealous of my rock star dad and his cool lifestyle.

I imagine helping to set up the instruments as the stadium fills with eager fans. I picture my dad giving me a huge hug and telling me how happy he is that I'm working with him. He sets up a stool for me on the side of the stage so that I can have the best view of the show. My heart pounds in anticipation as my dad and his bandmates test their instruments. The crowd starts cheering, anxious for them to get started. With the sound of the first notes, the crowd's screams become deafening. The steady, rhythmic drumbeats hypnotize the crowd and my body vibrates to the sound. I swell with pride watching my dad out there. His long brown hair is whipping around while he plays, his fingers gliding across the guitar. His tattered T-shirt reveals his muscular physique. He plays a solo for the audience and they go crazy for it. I clap frantically, and then he turns and winks at me. *That is MY dad!*

The sound of the bell ringing interrupts my daydream. The class empties out quickly. I hug my binder and follow suit, anxious to move on to the next class.

"Detention at lunch and after school, Miss Loewen," Mr. Letts reminds me. Luckily detention after school is only fifteen minutes. I won't be getting home too much later than usual.

At lunch, Amanda runs to me when she sees me at my locker.

"Let's go," she says.

"Can't," I tell her. "I got detention."

"What?! C'mon, Jayce. Just skip," she says.

"No, seriously, I can't. You guys go without me. I'm in for next time."

Amanda sticks out her bottom lip. "Fine. You better be coming tomorrow."

She waves at some of our other friends to follow her and they all come running. Amanda is on the SRC (Student Representative Council), so she knows a lot of people. Friends are one thing Amanda has never lacked. She's so much more outgoing than I am. I've always been the quieter one. I like having time to myself, and sometimes going out all the time with friends overwhelms me. The girls are always talking about things like hair and makeup and who is hooking up with whom. I mean, I care what I look like and everything, but I'm not obsessing. The constant gossip just wears me out. I'm always worrying about far more than having a bad hair day or who the latest crushes are. Often I feel like I'm on the outside looking in.

I watch as Amanda and the other girls laugh and head excitedly to the door. I think of them eating McDonald's and my stomach growls. I grab a notepad and head to detention. At least I can doodle or something while I'm there.

There are five other students in detention. Most of them are the burnouts of the school — the ones who clearly are about to be expelled. Some of them are pretty tough-looking, and they look me up and down as I take a seat.

I pretend to ignore their stares and flip open my notebook. I draw an outline of a woman's face and slowly begin adding features. Drawing has always been a love of mine, something I can get lost in for hours. Mom never had the money for us to be in any activities, so drawing was always something I could do whenever I wanted that didn't cost us any money.

"Pretty good," a husky voice says from behind me.

Startled, I flip my notebook shut quickly and spin on my seat. A tall boy with dark, shaggy hair is gazing at me intently. He has earrings in both of his ears and a huge tattoo of a dragon on his left forearm. He gives me a wide grin and I notice his bright white teeth.

"Whoa, settle down. No need to stop," he says, holding his hands up in the air.

"No need to spy on someone, either," I say back, shooting him a dirty look.

He seems amused by my answer. He still has a goofy grin on his face, and I can't help but notice that he has a dazzling smile.

"What are you in for?" he asks.

"Too many lates."

"What? Can't read a clock?" he says, mocking me.

"What? Can't mind your own business?" I retort.

He's holding a sandwich and staring at me instead of eating. Why can't he wipe that stupid grin off his face?

"I'm Kurt." He sticks out his hand for me to shake. I almost laugh at how absurd this is.

"Is this where you make all your friends, Kurt?"

He laughs out loud and flashes me another smile. Holy cow, his teeth are beautiful. In fact, once I get past his teeth, I see that he has really nice eyes, too. They're a hazel colour, and they're framed by thick, dark eyelashes. I wonder why I've never seen him around. Maybe this is where he spends all of his time.

"Jayce. Well, J.J., actually." I return his handshake. His hands are surprisingly soft and warm.

"I have a problem with being on time, too," Kurt says. "Well, actually, it's more like a problem with staying at school at all."

I nod. No wonder I've never seen him before. I gaze at his sandwich and my stomach growls.

"What grade are you in?" I ask.

"Grade twelve. But I'm not going to graduate." Kurt says this simply, as though it's not a big deal or anything. He finally takes a bite of his sandwich, and I'm relieved. If he eats it, I won't have to look at it anymore. "You?"

"Ten," I tell him. "But I have every intention of graduating on time."

He smiles his megawatt smile at me again. I seem to amuse him.

"Well, J.J., I bet you will."

He rises from the desk behind me and heads to the back of the room. I find myself blushing suddenly at our encounter and flip my notebook open to resume drawing. I try to concentrate, but my mind keeps playing our conversation, and his smile keeps interrupting my thoughts.

How crazy of this guy to just come up to me and start talking. I mean, I've never even seen him before. And in detention? It's probably not the best place to meet someone.

I continue my drawing, adding some shading, and I realize that, without even being conscious of it, I am drawing a picture of my mother. A younger, prettier version of her. The realization takes me by surprise, but it's undeniable. The thin, angular face and cheekbones. The perfect mane of hair. Her guarded smile. No matter what she is smiling about, the smile never quite reaches her eyes.

I add some finishing touches, and then the bell rings. The lunch hour is over. Kurt whisks past me and waves.

"See ya around," he says.

"Don't count on it," I say back. I don't know why I'm treating him like this, but I can't seem to help it. He laughs one more time and strides out of the classroom before I've even risen from my seat.

In the hallway I see Amanda and a crew of girls heading toward me.

"How was detention?" Amanda asks in a singsong voice.

"You missed out," I tell her, and she laughs.

"Well, we went to Wendy's. Erika Blackwell was there. You should have seen what she was wearing. Barely any clothes. She looked like a tramp. I just don't know what Luke sees in her, anyway."

Luke is Amanda's ex-boyfriend. They dated for all of three weeks before Luke hooked up with Erika at a party. Luke gave Amanda the cold shoulder after that night and has been with Erika ever since.

"He'd be so much happier with me," Amanda sighs.

"Maybe he's a dirtbag for cheating on you in the first place. You're better off without him," I tell her, but Amanda has this dreamy look on her face.

"We were perfect for each other," Amanda declares. "We could really talk. He told me things that nobody else knows. And I did the same. We had a connection."

"Amanda, he didn't even have the decency to face you and talk to you about what happened," I remind her. "He brushed you off."

"He's just confused right now," she tells me, and I roll my eyes. How can someone be so desperate for love that they can't see the situation for what it is? If a guy can't be dependable or there for you emotionally, how can you call that love?

The rest of the afternoon zips by, even detention after school. My eyes scan the room for Kurt, but he's nowhere in sight. I feel a pang of disappointment, and then tell myself that I'm being stupid. After telling Amanda that Luke isn't right for her, it seems funny that I'm even thinking of a boy I met in detention as boyfriend material.

I'm relieved when one of the teachers dismisses us. I'm anxious to get home and check on Joelle. I practically dive for the classroom doorway and dash for the school doors.

"What's the hurry?" I hear when I get outside. It's him. Kurt.

"I gotta get home," I say breathlessly, not even stopping to acknowledge him.

My stomach flutters a bit, knowing that he's nearby. I decide to turn to look at him and my insides almost melt at his dazzling smile. I notice his cool Converse shoes. He's wearing a leather jacket and he's standing all by himself. Has he been waiting for me?

"I'll walk you," he says. But I am still running. "Or run with you," he adds, laughing.

"Catch me if you can," I call out to him.

"Is that a challenge?" he asks. I'm secretly hoping he takes me up on it, and when I hear the sound of him approaching, I can't help but smile.

I give it all I've got, but his long legs are able to make bigger strides, and he keeps pace with me easily. We run side by side until we get close to my street, and then I slow to a walk.

"Wow, girl, you sure can run," he says admiringly. "What's the rush?"

I don't want to tell him about Joelle being practically by herself all day. I mean, my mom is there, but she isn't really able to care for her properly. What would I say?

My mom has kind of given up on everything and stays in bed all the time. My four-year-old sister pretty much fends for herself. I'd invite you in, except I'd have nothing to offer you but a hot, steamy bowl of oatmeal and, really, my life is getting far too complicated to add something new in, so it's best if we cut ties now.

Somehow I don't think that answer will work. I think quickly, hoping that I can come up with a convincing lie. "My grandma is coming in from out of town today. We've got to be at the bus depot to pick her up." The words fly out of my mouth before I have a chance to change them.

Oh no, surely he has no reason to go to the bus depot, does he?

Thankfully, my answer seems perfectly logical to him.

"So, you're not doing any more detention time, are you?" he asks. "You don't look like the type."

"What is that supposed to mean?" I snap back.

"Well, you just … I don't know … you seem really cool. I wouldn't have pegged you as someone who'd be getting detention."

"How would you know?" I say. His smile disappears.

"I'm not all bad, J.J.," he says pointedly. He seems reserved now, almost hurt. I try to look at his face, but he's staring at the ground. *He's tried to compliment me and I've shot him down.* Something about his clenched jaw and his downcast eyes makes me want to reach out and hug him.

"Sorry," I say softly, and instantly he brightens.

"It's all good," he replies. "People get the wrong idea about me all the time."

We walk in silence for a couple of minutes. I wipe the beads of sweat from my forehead. We're approaching my block. It's time to say goodbye. I don't want Kurt knowing where I live.

I look ahead and the first thing I notice is the police car and ambulance. They are in front of our house. My heart starts thudding in my chest. Joelle, my mother … what could have happened? The colour drains from my face and I break out into another run.

"J.J., what's the matter? Where are you going?" Kurt calls out, confused.

Kurt can't see where I live. He can't know what's going on. I lied about rushing home as it is.

"I gotta go. I'm way too late!" I call out. "I'll see you tomorrow!"

Kurt stops in his tracks. "Okay. I guess I'll see you tomorrow!" he calls back. He is oblivious to what is going on up the street from us.

I race down the street. My legs throb. I am filled with fear. A million different scenarios fill my mind, none of them good.

Of all of the days, why did I have to have detention today? Maybe if I hadn't been so late.

I look back again. Kurt has turned around to head back the way we came, and I feel some relief that he won't be part of whatever is waiting for me.

My eyes search for my mom or for Joelle as I approach our yard, but I see nothing. I race to the front door, which is wide open. I'm panting and sweating and out of breath. I feel like a crazed animal.

I zero in on the police officer who is kneeling by the couch. I realize that she is holding Joelle, who is crying.

"Ellie!" I call out to her, and she looks up in relief and runs to me, clutching me as hard as she can. I scoop her up and hold her close. "Where's Mom?" I ask, but Joelle has buried her head into my shoulder.

"We have another family member here!" the officer calls out. Two paramedics emerge, carrying a stretcher. Strapped inside is our mother. Her diminutive figure looks almost skeleton-like under the blankets. I can't really see her face beneath the oxygen mask, but I know it is most definitely her. I hold Joelle's head down on me so that she doesn't see our mother like this. The paramedics move quickly. I stand in confusion, trying to take in the scene. The police officer who was comforting Joelle starts asking questions, but her words blur together. The world feels like it is spinning out of control and the only thought that sticks with me is this: *I'm about to lose my mother.*

Chapter 2

I awake with a start to the sound of beeping monitors, a slow, steady rhythm. I open my eyes and bristle from the bright fluorescent lights above.

So it is all true. We are actually in the hospital. This wasn't a dream after all.

Mom is sleeping. Despite all of the tubes and things sticking out of her and how pale she looks, she seems to be resting comfortably. Ellie is sleeping, too. She's in the chair beside me, curled up into a ball. She looks so small and vulnerable, like a kitten. I stroke her forehead gently and then reach for my mom's hand.

Her hand is cold, her skin papery thin and almost translucent. *When did she get to be so frail?* I wonder. Seeing her this way, examining her up close, I can't believe how different she looks. Maybe I was just so busy trying to keep up with everything that I hadn't noticed. After all, Mom hasn't been feeling well for a long time. I think back to how many times I told her she should see a doctor.

"It's just a cold, Jayce," Mom kept assuring me.

"Mom, colds don't last this long," I'd say.

"I just got run down. That's all."

That's the thing: I'd had plenty of colds before but never one that had me in coughing fits like she'd have. Sometimes her long, hacking coughs would wake us up at night. Sometimes I'd rush into her room, asking if there was anything I could do. Her whole body would shake with each cough.

"I'm fine … fine," she'd assure me, waving me off. "Go back to sleep."

Now, I gaze at her face and a lump forms in my throat. *This isn't fine. Why didn't I make her do something about this sooner?* I smooth some of her hair back from her face.

Despite how different she looks, my mother is still beautiful. She's always been a head-turner. For as long as I can remember, men have openly stared at her. She is tall and thin, with long, curly blond hair that cascades halfway down her back, and she has huge blue eyes. I know she has always been proud of the attention. To her, her eyes are her best asset.

"'Those eyes can promise you the world ….' That's what your dad used to say to people about me." Mom would get a twinkle in her eye and a flush in her cheeks retelling the story.

When I was a young girl, Mom often talked to me about the magical love story between her and Dad. On special occasions, when Mom was getting ready to go out, I'd perch on the side of her bed and watch her apply her perfume and makeup, mesmerized by her beauty. I'd look at her in wonder, thinking that I'd never seen someone so beautiful. Except then Dad stopped coming around as much, and everything was different. Mom didn't dress up and go out at night much after that, but she kept telling me that he'd be coming back soon.

"Life on the road is busy, you know, Jayce," she'd say to me, when I asked when I'd see him next. "Your dad is an amazing musician. He's gotta be out there playing if he's going to make it big. And your dad, he's going to be real big someday."

Mom never stopped believing that he was out there working hard for us and that he'd be back. But he only came back once in a while and often for only one night at a time. He'd call unexpectedly to let us know he'd be coming into town. She'd start humming or singing around the house when she knew he was coming. She'd often spend hours cooking food so that she could spoil him with delicious meals, and she'd scrub the house until not a speck of dirt remained.

We'd be practically buzzing with excitement when we'd hear the familiar rumble of his big van coming up the street. I'd light up like a Christmas tree when I saw him. He'd scoop me up and twirl me around and I'd feel so loved and protected when he put his big, strong arms around me. He had his own special name for me: "Jaybird." He'd also pick my mom off her feet and swing her around. Mom would blush and hit him playfully, but I could tell she loved it.

I wish I had more memories of him, but, in truth, I only got to be with him for a few hours at a time on the days he came home. Mom would put me to bed early so that the two of them could go out. When I woke up in the morning, I'd run to check if he was still around. I'd see them tangled in each other's arms in bed, and my heart would swell with pride, seeing my parents together like a real family. I'd hope and pray that he'd stick around for longer, but when they awoke, he'd usually start packing his bag. He'd explain that he had to get back on the road. I could see the disappointment on my mom's face each time, because it mirrored my own.

As I got older, it got harder to keep feeling so good about him. I'd see my friends with their dads, playing catch or going to the store together, and my heart hurt thinking about mine. I'd tell everyone that he was on tour, but when he didn't come back for months at a time, my friends started wondering if he even existed. In grade seven, after not seeing my dad for over a year, I started wondering if he even existed, too. And if he really loved us, why wasn't he here with us?

"Your birthday is coming up, J.J.," Mom had remarked to me one morning, just a couple of weeks before my twelfth birthday.

"Yeah," I'd said noncommittally.

"How about we have a nice get-together for you and your friends in the backyard?" she'd offered.

I'd shrugged. Our lawn was so overgrown and the weeds were so high, it looked like a jungle back there. Then there was the car — the metal heap of junk that stood out like a sore thumb. It wasn't the party atmosphere I wanted. Sensing my displeasure, Mom had sighed.

"Jayce, your friends aren't going to care about what the yard looks like. They'll be here to celebrate you."

"I'll just tell them to bring their safari equipment. It'll be great," I'd said sarcastically.

Mom had thrown down the fork she was holding with such force that it had bounced loudly across the table.

"Is there a problem with the life I've made for you?" she'd asked, stern.

"Life is perfect," I'd replied. "What more could I want?" I knew with my bad attitude I was about to push my mom over the edge.

"If there is something you feel you're really lacking, let's hear it!" she'd barked.

"How about a father?" I'd shot back.

Mom's face had changed. She'd pursed her lips tightly and taken a deep breath.

"You have a father, J.J. He loves you very much. He loves both of us. He just can't be here as much as he'd like." Even Mom had known that her words sounded hollow.

"As much as he'd like? How about ever?!" I'd yelled.

"Is that what this is about?" Mom had spat. "Your dad will be at your birthday."

"How can you be so sure? He wasn't at my last birthday."

That was the truth. I had waited all day for him to come, thinking there was no way he'd miss my important day, but he'd never shown up. Mom had bitten her nails nervously as the day had gone on, knowing I was only half-interested in the small party I was having. I'd watched the window like a hawk. I'd been sure he was just late, that something must have kept him. But he never showed up. There wasn't even a phone call.

A year later, Mom had tried to convince me he wouldn't fail me again.

"He'll be there," Mom had assured me, her voice softer.

"I'll believe it when I see it," I'd said, running from the room to fight the tears that pricked my eyelids.

When the day of my party had rolled around, I'd woken up in a foul mood. Mom had put a plastic table-cloth on our rotting picnic table and had brought out a mishmash of dishes for our guests. She'd made a chocolate cake with thick chocolate frosting, and it looked delicious. She'd counted out twelve candles for the cake.

"I don't have an extra one for good luck, but you don't need it, J.J."

I'd known she was trying to reassure me, but I had felt like I needed all the luck I could get. Mom had been overenthusiastic about the whole party, wanting to make the day special for me, but all I'd been able to think of was how everything we had wasn't good enough. I'd been worried that my friends would notice that my party looked nothing like their parties, where there were tons of decorations, games, and food, and everything looked picture-perfect.

And all I'd been able to think about was how my dad wasn't going to be there and how awful it made me feel. As though Mom could read my mind, she'd kept saying, "He'll be here, J.J., you'll see."

When my guests had arrived, Mom had poured them tall glasses of iced tea and fawned over their outfits. Nobody had seemed to mind how ugly our backyard was or how plain the party was. But I'd sat sullen, unable to shake the disappointment of my father not showing up. Didn't he know how important birthdays were? And, of all birthdays, this one?

I have friends here who think you don't even exist! I wanted to scream.

"Why don't we open gifts?" Mom had said brightly. She'd gathered the gifts and set them before me. I'd stared at them without moving. My friends had shifted uncomfortably in their seats, wondering why I looked so miserable.

"Go on, Jayce," Mom had said, her tone serious. She'd given me a look to tell me to smarten up, but I hadn't cared.

I'd started ripping bright red wrapping paper off one of the gifts, but I hadn't been able to muster the energy to look excited. Underneath the paper there had been a jewellery box covered in bright pink velvet. It had fake jewels glued on the top. It was from Monica, a girl I'd gone to school with since kindergarten.

"That is SO beautiful!" my mom had oozed. She'd squeezed Monica's shoulders affectionately. The girls had oohed and aahed at my gift.

"Do you like it?" Monica had asked. She'd seemed puzzled by my lack of reaction to what everyone else thought was such a nice gift. I hadn't meant to be so disrespectful, I really hadn't, but all I could think about was how badly I wanted another life. One with a nice house and a pretty yard. One with a dad.

I'd pursed my lips together when I'd started to feel them tremble, but the flood of emotion had been too strong. I'd burst into tears.

"Mmm ... maybe we should go," Jaclyn had suggested. Everyone had looked very uncomfortable. Even my mom couldn't keep acting as though everything was okay. All at once the girls had started to rise from the table and gather their things. A pile of presents sat unopened on the table. Even the cake was untouched, the candles unlit.

"Are you sure, girls? We haven't even had cake!" Mom had said, with panic in her voice.

"How could someone be so ungrateful?" I'd heard Monica say as they walked toward the gate. Amanda had slowed her pace and turned toward me while the other girls continued walking.

"Yeah, and see? I told you she didn't have a dad!" Jaclyn had added.

I'd wanted to sink into the ground. I'd wanted to die from embarrassment. I'd wanted to scream as loud as I could from all the hurt I was feeling. Instead, I'd sobbed uncontrollably.

"Thank you for coming, girls!" Mom had called after them as they'd hurried out of the yard, grateful to be leaving. Then Mom had picked up the torn wrapping paper from the grass and stuffed it into a plastic bag. Amanda had stayed back to help her.

"Thank you, Amanda," Mom had said. Amanda had ran up to me and whispered sorry and patted my back before heading back home, but I hadn't been able to say anything.

"I'll just go and get these glasses washed up," Mom had said to me gently.

I'd nodded through my sobs, unable to stop the flood of tears.

"Where's my little Jaybird?" Dad's familiar voice had called out from the entrance of the gate. Mom had run out of the house toward him, throwing her arms around him.

"Eleanor," he'd breathed as he held her close. "Have I missed you." I could just feel her excitement at being in his arms. They'd stood in a tight embrace for several moments.

"Jayce —" Mom had turned in my direction, leading Dad toward me. She'd glowed with happiness. "I told you he'd be here."

My dad had released his grip on my mom's hand and had come toward me with his arms outstretched.

"Why in the world is my baby girl crying on her birthday?" he'd said, his eyebrows furrowed with concern. He'd stood waiting for me to jump into his arms like always, but I just couldn't do it. Not this time.

"You're too late!" I'd shrieked.

I'd stormed past him and run into the house. I'd gone straight to my room and slammed the door. He'd come after me and grabbed me before I could make it to my bed.

"I'm here, J.J.," he'd reminded me. He'd put his arms around me and squeezed me tight, sending me back into uncontrollable sobs. I'd wanted to hit him, push him away, and make him feel like garbage for not being around. But it didn't matter how mad I was. The feel of his strong arms around me, holding me tight, and the smell of him, had made me crumple in defeat. No matter how desperately I'd wanted to hate him, I couldn't. *I actually have a dad. And he's here. Finally.*

"Has she woken up yet?"

My thoughts are broken by the sound of someone's voice. It's a nurse, coming to check my mother's vitals. I rub my eyes and sit straighter in my seat as I watch her.

"She's been like this for hours," I tell the nurse. She's middle-aged, plump, and pretty. She gives me a sympathetic smile as she gingerly lifts Mom's arm to take her blood pressure.

"Rest is really important for her right now."

"Is she in any pain?"

"I think she's comfortable," the nurse assures me. "I'll be back to check on her again in a little while. Remember to buzz the nurse's station if you need anything." She holds the buzzer out for me to see, and I nod. She writes information on the clipboard at the edge of the bed.

Joelle stirs from her sleep on the chair and stretches her limbs. Her hair has come loose from its ponytail and tendrils of curls sprout from every direction.

"J.J., I'm hungry," Joelle whines. I try to smooth her hair back.

"I know, honey." We haven't brought any food with us and I have no money.

"Would you like some toast?" the nurse asks. "I can make some for you in the kitchen."

Joelle nods and leaps off the chair. "Can I come with you?" she asks with her dazzling smile.

"Of course, sweetie pie." The nurse smiles. She holds out her hand for Joelle to take it and Joelle does so without hesitation.

"I better come, too," I say. I don't want to let Joelle out of my sight right now. There's no telling what she might say to one of the hospital staff.

Together, we walk down the hallway to the kitchen.

"Help yourself, too, honey," she says to me, taking out a loaf of bread. "Can I leave you to prepare it?"

"Sure," I say.

I put two slices of bread in the toaster. Despite the trauma of the day, my stomach growls at the smell of the toast. Joelle pulls out little packages of butter and jam from a bowl on the counter. When the toast pops, she rubs her hands in anticipation.

I pass the toast to her and decide to make some for myself. I have no idea how long we'll be here and fresh, warm food would be a welcome taste. We stand in the kitchen, chewing greedily. I take a paper Dixie cup from the cup dispenser and fill it with cold water from the tap. We take turns sipping the water as we chew our toast.

"Can I have more, please?" Joelle asks. I don't want to eat too much of the hospital's food, especially since we aren't even patients here, but I also don't know when we'll be going home and when we'll eat next.

"One more slice each," I agree.

We finish our third slices and wash our hands in the sink. I wipe the counter to clean away any crumbs, and together Joelle and I head back toward Mom's room. We hear voices as we approach.

"Do you have family you can call? Is there another relative who can take care of the girls?" The voice belongs to a doctor standing next to Mom's bed.

"I have a sister who lives close by. She'll come and stay at the house," is Mom's hoarse reply.

My heart thumps in my chest. Mom doesn't have a sister. At least, not one I've ever met. We enter the room and I look at my mom wide-eyed. She looks at me, but doesn't bat an eye.

"Would you like one of the nurses to call her for you?" the doctor offers.

"I can call her myself," Mom says.

I stand, confused. *What does Mom mean? And why does someone have to come and take care of us?* The doctor sees us and smiles.

"Very well, then. It's important that you make those arrangements right away."

Mom nods and smiles sweetly at the doctor. She waits for him to leave before smiling at me.

"Mom, what's going on?" I say, panic creeping into my voice.

"Jayce, we need to talk," Mom says seriously. "Shut the door."

I close the door to her room while Joelle races to sit on the bed next to Mom. She clings to her and Mom strokes her forehead, brushing Joelle's crazy curls from her face. Sensing something awful, my stomach churns and my heart thuds wildly in my chest.

"I'm sick," Mom says simply. "Really sick." Her voice is barely a whisper.

I flop onto the chair beside the bed, and all the air seems to get sucked from my lungs in a split second.

"I know, but you'll be better before you know it."

"I'm not sure this time, J.J."

"What do you mean, you're not sure?"

"It's not that simple. I've got a mass — on my lungs. It … it …" A sob erupts from her. It's deep and aching and I can feel her fear. "It's cancer."

"What?!" I shriek. "How?! You're supposed to have a bad cold. You said so yourself."

Joelle hums to herself, oblivious to what Mom's words mean.

"I'm afraid not," Mom says gently.

"So, what does this mean?" I bark. "You're gonna …" I can't even bring myself to say the word. Especially not with Ellie right here. I mean, cancer? The only people I've ever known to have cancer are Terry Fox and Amanda's grandpa, and they died. *Died.*

"I'll fight this, but it is stage four already. That means it's pretty advanced."

I stand stunned. Her words are like a punch to the stomach. Suddenly I regret the toast I've eaten, because I feel like I'm going to vomit. Joelle plays with Mom's fingers and continues humming, filling the awkward silence between us.

"J.J., things are going to be fine," Mom says reassuringly, but I'm no idiot.

"No, they're not!" I stammer. "How can you say that? And you don't have a sister who lives nearby, so what is that all about?"

Mom clears her throat and rubs her eyes.

"The hospital wants to know that there will be a caregiver at the house," Mom explains. "Both for you guys and for me."

"But I can do that!" I protest.

"There will be lots of medications. It's not going to be easy," Mom says.

"It's fine. I can do it! I take care of so much already!"

"I can't afford a caregiver," Mom replies. "But the hospital wants to know that I'll be discharged into someone's care. A sixteen-year-old doesn't count."

"But we don't have an aunt," I remind her.

"The hospital doesn't need to know that."

"You're *lying*? And we do so have caregivers. What about Mrs. Johnson? Can't she watch you *and* Ellie? Or what about Dad?"

Mom glances at me wistfully. "That is my plan, Jayce, to track down your dad and have him come."

I nod, numb.

"Mommy, when can we go home?" Joelle interrupts.

"Soon, Ellie, soon," Mom purrs at her. Joelle snuggles back into her.

"Why not now?" she whines.

"Mommy needs a bit more rest," Mom explains.

"But I wanna go NOW!" she pouts.

"I can just take her, Mom. We'll take the bus back for tonight and return in the morning."

Mom looks back and forth at the two of us, deciding what to do.

"What about school? What about Ellie?" Mom asks.

Ugh. The thought of having to go to school tomorrow is unbearable. But if I don't go, the school will call.

"I'll handle it," I say. I have no idea how I'm going to handle it.

"Get me my purse," she says, and I reach for her purse in the cupboard beside her bed. "Here are the bus passes." She hesitates before passing them over. "Oh, J.J., I just don't know."

The doctor enters the room again. He glances at his watch and looks at Ellie.

"Almost time for bed, isn't it, little one?" he says. Mom and I exchange nervous glances.

"We're just on our way," I say brightly, reaching for Joelle. "Our aunt is waiting in the lobby. She had to park in the front loop, so we have to run down and meet her before she gets a ticket." The story tumbles out of my mouth before I can stop. How can lying come to me so easily? The doctor seems satisfied with this and Mom gives me a grateful smile.

Ellie follows me and blows Mom a kiss. Although she's used to spending a lot of time with me while Mom is at work, she definitely recognizes that there is more going on here than usual. I can feel her apprehension at leaving the hospital without Mom.

Ellie falls asleep on the bus ride home. When we

reach our stop, I scoop her up from the seat, and she barely flinches. By the time I reach our front door, my arms are shaking from the strain of carrying her and sweat is dripping from my forehead. I transfer her to one of my shoulders so that I can fumble for my house key, and luckily I make it inside without disturbing her. I manage to slip off her shoes with one hand and decide that she can just sleep in her clothes. I quickly place her in her bed and kiss her cheek.

Poor Ellie. She has no real clue about what is going on and what is going to happen to Mom. How do we even explain this to her?

I return to the living room and turn on the TV. I can't seem to concentrate on anything, but it's nice to have the background noise and something to distract my thoughts. Hanging over the arm of the couch is Mom's sweater. I grab it like it's my lifeline and hug it tight. I take a deep breath, inhaling her scent, and the familiarity of it sends me into sobs.

What if I lose her? Oh, God. I can't lose her. She's my mother. We're too young to lose our mother. I wrap myself in her sweater, desperate for some comfort. *Mom is going to need me to be strong. She needs me to take care of things.* I let my body unleash all of the terror and sadness I'm feeling. I roll into a ball and cry until my head throbs and there's nothing left.

I can do this. I can be strong for everyone.

Just not tonight.

Chapter 3

This may sound crazy, but Joelle has never met our dad. The night of my twelfth birthday, after my party fell apart and Dad showed up late, Dad ended up staying for four whole nights. It was enough time that I even got my hopes up that he might be staying with us for good, but I should've known better. On the fourth night I overheard my parents talking. It sounded tense and heated. I tiptoed to my doorway so I could make out what they were saying.

"We can't keep doing this, Joe." Mom sounded tired. "We keep waiting around for you, and for what?"

"What do you mean, for what? What is that supposed to mean?"

"We need more than this. We want you to stay. Jayce deserves to have her father around."

"You know how it is, Eleanor."

"No, I don't. Not anymore. I think you owe us more than a few nights and a cheque once in a while."

It got quiet.

"That's how you see me?" Dad's voice was sharp.

"I think it's time you make a decision. Us or the band." Mom's words made my stomach flop. I crossed my fingers and shut my eyes tight. I held my breath, hoping he'd agree to stay.

"Eleanor ..."

"I mean it." It was silent again, until I heard the kitchen chair leg scrape against the floor, and then footsteps. I ran back to my bed and pulled the covers over myself, but my heart was pounding. I heard Mom's bedroom door close and I knew that she'd left Dad in the kitchen.

The next morning I woke up to find Mom wiping her tears at the kitchen table. Dad's shoes were missing from the front door. My heart dropped.

A few months later, Mom announced that she was pregnant. Joelle was born exactly nine months after my twelfth birthday. In a way, I suppose she was the best thing to come out of that day. Mom tried to get a hold of Dad for months to let him know that they were expecting another child, but she couldn't reach him. She tried calling the numbers of different places she knew he'd stayed at in the past, but no one would tell her where Dad was or how to contact him.

When Joelle arrived, she was a welcome addition to our family. She brought me and Mom so much joy. I knew it hurt Mom terribly that my dad had no idea he had another daughter. Sometimes I'd see her wiping tears as she rocked Joelle to sleep.

In the end, Mom gave up trying to find him. I just kept feeling angry that he was missing so much. Yeah, he'd missed so much with me, but with Joelle being a helpless little baby, it seemed doubly unfair to her. I was already used to it.

At school I'd google "Raven's Spell" and try to figure out where he was. Maybe I could convince him to come home, and Mom wouldn't have to do everything herself. I could never find current touring information, only old dates from years past. I'd see pictures of him online from various gigs or band cover shots. His eyes were often closed, and he was always smiling widely while he played his guitar. Seeing his picture was both comforting and painful. It was reassuring to know he still existed, but it was never enough. It was mental torture, the feeling of wanting something so badly that I knew I couldn't have. And knowing that he'd chosen to have it this way — that was a whole other kind of hurt altogether.

Dad never showed up again. Not even for one night.

He chose the band. No matter how much time passes, that still feels like a punch to the gut. *He doesn't even know that Joelle exists.* My hands ball into fists. *He'll get to know her now,* I tell myself. *We'll find him.* But how will we find him? And what if he is hiding from us on purpose? What if he doesn't want to be found? What then?

As the morning sun floods the kitchen, I rummage through the junk drawer, hoping to come upon Mom's address book. Surely I'll be able to track Dad down. I mean, someone must know something about where he is. And, once he knows the situation, he'll realize how much help we need and he'll step in. He's going to have to stand up and be a man and take care of his family.

I want to believe this so badly — that he'll step in and make things okay. But it's hard to imagine this, since he hasn't been around in years. Really, I was hoping that I'd wake up this morning and Mom would be fixing us breakfast, or that I'd at least hear her coughing in her bed. Her absence is unnerving, and it reminds me that the nightmare of what's happening is all true.

Where is the book? I can't make any calls without trying the numbers in Mom's book. I wouldn't know where to start otherwise.

"What are you doing?" Ellie asks. She has come into the kitchen, clutching her threadbare yellow blanket and sucking her thumb.

"Just looking for something. You need to go and get dressed."

"Why?" Ellie asks.

"What do you mean, why? I have to go to school and you're going to Mrs. Johnson's."

"What about Mom?" Ellie whimpers.

"She has to stay in the hospital a little longer. She told us that." I know I should be comforting her and soothing her jagged nerves, but I'm so preoccupied with finding Mom's address book that worrying about Ellie is too much for the moment.

"But I want Mom," Ellie cries. She puts her thumb back in her mouth, sucking even harder than before.

"She'll be home soon," I snap. "Now go get dressed."

I've emptied out almost all of the contents of the drawer, but the address book is not there. Frustrated, I throw everything back into the drawer, and slide it closed with my hip. *Mom's room? Maybe it's in there.*

As I head toward Mom's room, I'm happy to see that Ellie is pulling a shirt over her head. I flick on the light to Mom's bedroom. She rarely turns on the light or takes the blanket off the window, so it's weird to see the room bathed in light. It smells musty and gross to me. I wonder if the pungent odour is of illness, if the cancer was even seeping through her skin without us noticing. The bed is a tangled mess of sheets and blankets, and a glass of water sits half-full on the bedside table.

I open the top drawer of her dresser first, where she keeps her underwear and socks. Mom has always told me to keep important documents like my birth certificate and immunization record in my underwear drawer, because I'll always remember to look there first. I rummage through her undergarments and find a couple of black-and-white photos that must be her as a young girl, but nothing else.

I survey the room.

I open the closet door, but the closet is mostly empty, except for a few items of clothing on hangers. Mom's worn, stained running shoes that she wears to the diner are at the bottom of her closet, along with her work uniform and apron. The plastic name tag is facing up; *Eleanor* is written on it in black letters.

"Ellie, are you ready yet?" I call out, hoping that Ellie hasn't become preoccupied with her toys or something else. I get on my hands and knees to look under the bed. There are a couple of old candy wrappers, a receipt, and balls of dust, but no address book.

I place my hands in between the box spring and the mattress, hoping that perhaps Mom has hidden the book there. I've seen people hide things in between their mattresses on TV. Mostly money or weapons, of course, but you never know. I slide my hands underneath the mattress and feel my way around the silky fabric, but come up empty-handed. *Where could it be?*

One look at the clock, and I know that I must get Ellie to Mrs. Johnson's and get myself to school. I hit the light switch in Mom's room and grab my backpack. After school, we'll head back to the hospital and Mom will be able to tell me where it is. Then I can start making phone calls and Dad will come. He'll take care of everything.

Chapter 4

By some miracle, I make it in to class on time. I'm sweating, both from rushing and from the anxiety of our secret. Will Joelle be able to keep our secret from Mrs. Johnson? How can I trust a four-year-old to keep quiet about the fact that our mother is lying in a hospital bed right now? That's pretty monumental. Not only that, I have to worry about how I'm going to keep everything together until Mom gets better and comes home to us. She's counting on me.

"Are you okay?" Amanda asks.

"Yeah. Why?" I shrug.

"You just seem weird today."

I know that this is the part when I should confide in her, given that she is my best friend, but I just can't bring myself to say anything. I watch as she scrapes old nail polish from her fingernails and holds her fingers out to examine them and I can't help but feel that as much as Amanda is my friend, she just won't get it. Like the time

I tried to explain that I couldn't come on the year-end camping trip because we couldn't afford the fees or the supplies. I had wanted to go so badly, but there was no way Mom could make it happen. When I told Amanda, she got really upset with me as though I was staying home on purpose. She didn't talk to me for a week. She was upset at me for leaving her to go on the trip alone, without a best friend, even though she knew I couldn't afford to go and there were thirty-seven other students going. She'd even threatened to get a new best friend, but then came around one day and apologized. Truth be told, sometimes Amanda isn't really good at seeing beyond what affects her.

Mr. Letts enters the room and nods in my direction. I can tell he is happy to see me in class on time. I shrink into my seat and hope that I can fly under the radar today. Mr. Letts writes the same heading on the board as he did yesterday:

TAKE YOUR SON OR DAUGHTER TO WORK DAY

Ha. Yesterday I was wishing Mom had a better job, something more glamorous. Today I just wish she could go to work. The familiar feeling of guilt creeps over me. How could I be embarrassed of her and her job, when all she's done is work hard to try and support us? And me commenting that she was missing all these days at work as though it was out of laziness or something, when really she was being attacked by some terrible illness. She was dying! I feel sick to myself, thinking of how selfish I've been.

What will I do about Monday? If I talk to Mr. Letts about it, he'll know my mom is sick. No one can know this. If other people know she's actually in the hospital, who knows what will happen to me and Ellie. Maybe I can pretend she's only sick for that day and I can ask if I can go with Amanda to her dad's work. He is an accountant at an office downtown. I'm sure his office wouldn't mind a second tagalong.

Mr. Letts did say that we could choose a relative or a neighbour, but that doesn't help me, either. Mrs. Johnson is too old to hold a job other than taking care of Ellie, and I don't have any other relatives around. That's another thing. Not only is my father not around, but I have no idea what my mother's side of the family is like, either. All I know is that Mom left the town she grew up in at a young age and never looked back. I don't even know if she's ever spoken to her mother since. Mom has always been very quiet about her family, and changes the subject whenever it comes up.

Maybe Mom's family could help us? Maybe I should just talk to Mom about it and see what she says. This is no time to pretend that everything is going to be okay.

"Miss Loewen, is there something more interesting on your mind than English Language Arts this morning?" Mr. Letts asks me pointedly.

Giggles erupt in the room and everyone stares at me. I feel my cheeks burn with embarrassment and shake my head.

"I'm paying attention," I assure him. He stares at me for a moment and then continues on with the lesson. The palms of my hands are sweating. I rub them on my jeans and try to focus. Mr. Letts is saying that he wants us to keep a journal for class, and that he'll reply to our entries each week.

"The contents of the journals will remain confidential. I want you to practise writing about things that are important to you in these books." He holds up a stack of cheap spiral notebooks. "Maybe you want to write about your hobby of car restoration, or about something else you're passionate about. Maybe you want to vent about some of the injustices you see in the world. Maybe you'll write about where you see your future going: your hopes and dreams. You get the idea."

He walks down the aisles and hands a notebook to each student.

"I want a minimum of three-quarters of a page written each week. The notebooks are to be handed in every Friday and I will return them to you on Monday. Understood?"

There is a collective groan from the class.

I open my notebook and stare at the blank page before me. It looks overwhelming. *Write about what's important to me? Are you serious? Where do I start?* We've been in survival mode for so long, I don't even know how to answer. Why do some people have to struggle more than others? Why does my mom have to work so hard and yet we barely have food to eat? Why does she have to deal with this illness now? And what's going to become of me and Ellie if she can't beat this?

Hobbies or passions? Drawing, I guess. But I don't want to write about that. I'd rather just do it. Not that I have time for it now anyhow. Injustices? Plenty. Where you see your future going? At this point, wherever it's going, it is not looking promising. I honestly can't imagine what I'll write.

"Jayce," Amanda whispers to me from across the aisle. I glance at her quickly, hoping that Mr. Letts doesn't call me out again.

"Lunch?" she asks. I have no money again, and I just know that they're heading back to a fast food restaurant. Ever since Amanda got a car, my group of friends goes every day. I shake my head no and Amanda's lips purse in frustration.

"Fine. Come to my house after school," she whispers. That I can't do for sure. I have to get home as soon as I can to pick up Joelle and get back to the hospital.

"Lunch," I decide, and she brightens up instantly. Already my stomach is growling and it's nine in the morning. Sitting with my friends while they eat will feel like torture, but I can tell that Amanda is no longer irritated. Right now, with everything falling apart, her not being pissed at me just makes things easier.

When the lunch hour rolls around, Amanda and I head to her car where Jenna and Danika are already waiting. They give me a polite smile, but seem irritated that I'm joining them.

"Shotgun!" Jenna shouts. Danika pouts at her and reaches for the handle of one of the back doors.

"Fine," Danika says. "But I get it on the way back."

"J.J. gets shotgun," Amanda states, and both girls groan. I smile at Amanda gratefully and feel proud that she's chosen me over them. I mean, I am her best friend and everything, but I haven't been around a whole lot lately. I slide into the seat and buckle my seatbelt. I spot a toonie on the floor near my foot. It'll only take us a few minutes to get to the restaurant. Perhaps I could scoop up the money and use it for a cheeseburger — that way, I'll be eating something, too. Maybe I could replace the money tomorrow, and just throw it back onto the floor and she won't even know. We start driving, and it isn't long before the telltale golden arches come into view.

"You think Erika will be here?" Amanda asks us.

"If she is, you should totally snub her off again," Jenna says.

Amanda laughs. "I mean, who does she think she is? I hope Luke is here. I'm wearing his favourite shirt." Her T-shirt is fitted and low cut, accentuating her breasts and her petite figure.

"You don't really want him back, do you?" I ask. "He cheated on you, Amanda."

"Well, things weren't going perfect. I made mistakes; we didn't get a chance to work it out."

"So he can just go be with someone else?" I demand.

"You just don't get it, J.J. It's not like you've ever been in love."

Danika and Jenna nod. They've had boyfriends. They support Amanda trying to get Luke back.

Amanda's got me there. I've never been in love. I've never had a date. No first kiss. Nothing. My parents' relationship wasn't the norm, either, so what do I know?

We pull into the parking lot. I look down at the toonie again, second-guessing what I should do, but then decide that I'll leave the money in the car after all. We get in the restaurant and line up at the till. I tell the girls to go ahead of me and then distance myself from the line. Amanda orders and then turns to talk to me and sees that I'm across the room.

"J.J.? What's up?" she calls. I shrug and tell her I'm not hungry. She turns back to the cashier and waits for her meal. When she has her order, she walks over to me and I can't help but stare at her food. She has two cheeseburgers, an order of small fries, and a medium drink, and her food smells delicious.

"Let's go sit," she says. The other girls are still in line.

"Should we wait?"

"No, come on!"

I follow her up the stairs to the seating area. Once she picks a table, she tosses me a cheeseburger.

"Let's share," she says.

I think of protesting and giving her another lame excuse, but I'm so hungry that I decide to take the burger. "Well, maybe I should eat something," I reply, feigning indifference.

Danika and Jenna join us with their trays of food.

"You will not believe who is downstairs right now!" Danika says.

"Who?" Amanda replies, absently. She's shoving french fries in her mouth in quick succession.

"Errriiikkkaaa," Jenna pipes in, in a singsong voice.

"No flippin' way!" Amanda's eyes grow large and suddenly angry.

"Oh, yeah. And Luke's there, too."

Amanda straightens in her seat, smooths her bangs, and fluffs the bottom of her hair.

"Oh, we are so done here," she announces.

Danika and Jenna have barely opened their food, and Amanda is rising from her seat, clearly ready to leave. "Let's go," she commands. I look at Danika and Jenna, and they dutifully wrap up their meals to take with them. I've finished my cheeseburger, so I guess I'm ready to go, too.

Amanda sips on her drink as we head toward the staircase. I want to ask her what the big deal is — why can't we just sit and eat lunch together without worrying about Luke and Erika being in the same building? But apparently being in the same building outside of school isn't allowed, because Amanda is hightailing it toward the front entrance and the food counter where customers place their orders. Danika and Jenna struggle to carry their meals in their hands. We turn toward the entrance, and there they are. Luke and Erika. Holding hands and kissing while they wait in the long lineup. Amanda makes a sound at the sight of them — almost like a squeak. Almost like she didn't expect that they'd have their arms around each other, let alone be making out right here in plain view.

I watch as she marches toward them, and before I have a chance to stop her, she flings her cup at them, sending her pop cascading down the sides of their snuggled bodies.

They look up in surprise to Amanda smiling.

"Oops," she says sweetly. "I guess I tripped."

If looks could kill, Luke's eyes would bury her in seconds. Erika just looks stunned and a little scared.

I feel bad for them, even though I know Amanda is my best friend and I should be on her side right now. It's just that this seemed … I don't know … a little unnecessary. A little mean. Danika and Jenna high-five her and laugh their heads off and head back out to the car. Amanda and I follow. I'm not laughing, and Amanda knows it. She looks at me pointedly and then says to Danika, "You get shotgun this time."

I climb in the back with Jenna and stare out the window. Amanda glances at me periodically through the rear-view mirror. Even though I don't meet her eyes, I can tell she's staring at me. I glance out the window, thinking that, for once, I'm actually embarrassed to be with these girls. I know Amanda feels hurt about the breakup, but throwing pop on people doesn't seem like a cool move. But then I remember how I almost took a toonie from her today so that I could eat, and how she ended up sharing her lunch with me, and I feel shame. Who am I to judge? Maybe I'm just taking everything a little too seriously. Maybe I just have to lighten up.

During fourth period our class heads to the library. I snag a computer before they are all taken. Although we're supposed to be working on our social studies assignments, I want to try looking up my dad again. I feel sick as I type his name and his band into the search engine. It's been a long time since I've tried looking him up. Once again I'm met with the same pictures I remember studying when I was younger. I see that Raven's Spell was nominated for a

Juno Award in 2004. I see old tour dates until 2007, but nothing dated past that point. *This can't be right.* Did the band change their name? Did he join another band? Why is there no current information for him? There has to be some kind of explanation. If he was as successful as he was made out to be, why can't I find him?

I see information for other Joe Loewens: one is a doctor, one is an accountant. I see that there are Facebook profiles I could search, but we're not allowed to access Facebook on the school computers, and Mr. Mitchell, our social studies teacher, always keeps a close eye on the computer stations.

I scroll through a couple more pages, hoping to come upon something that catches my eye, but nothing does. I don't have time to write down all of the Loewens that are listed in Canada, but I try to copy as many as I can. The class goes by quickly; by the time the bell goes, I've only managed to write down the information for eight Loewens. It's a start.

"Got time to hang out?" Kurt walks up to me as the last bell rings.

"No, sorry," I say. "I've got to get home."

"Right. Your grandma's in town," he nods, remembering our conversation after school yesterday. "Can I walk you?" he asks. I want so badly to say yes but a leisurely stroll isn't really how I was planning on getting home. A marathon sprint was more like it.

"Well, I'm kinda in a hurry. Another day?"

"Oh, so you want to race again?" His eyes are dancing, his smile wide.

"Not exactly, Kurt."

"That's cool. I gotta get home, too." He's grinning at me from ear to ear. It makes me want to drop everything to spend some time with this guy, but I can't.

"Here's my number," he says, handing me a folded piece of paper. "Give me a call." He seems so confident and self-assured, but not in an egotistical kind of way. It's like he just marches to the beat of his own drum and doesn't care what anyone else thinks of him.

I take the paper and nod. "Thanks. I will." And I mean it. "Talk to you later," I tell him, and then I turn on my heels to go. As I head out to the street, I spot Amanda, Danika, and Jenna. They are huddled close together, but they are staring at me. Amanda looks up and breaks the huddle as I get closer to them.

"Well, well … who's that?" she asks.

"A friend," I reply.

"I've never seen him before. Is he new?"

"No."

"He seemed pretty into you."

"Whatever," I say.

"What's with the one-word answers?" Amanda's eyebrows are knitted together, her lips pursed. I simply shrug.

"What's with his weird clothes?" Danika pipes in. And then the three of them laugh. So that's what they were doing. Sizing him up when they saw us talking. I don't think his clothes are weird at all. In fact, I love how he seems so comfortable in his own skin.

"I know, right? Ever heard of a haircut? And who wears leather jackets anymore?" Amanda adds.

"I gotta go," I say. Not only am I anxious to get Ellie and get to the hospital, but this conversation is irritating me.

"Oh, right." Amanda rolls her eyes at me, as though whatever I need to do couldn't possibly be important. Little does she know just how important it is. What is her problem? I feel like she's a step away from losing it on me, and I'm not sure why.

"See ya," she says. She wraps her arms around Danika and Jenna and pulls them off toward the school. It makes me feel small, watching them walk off together.

I sling my backpack over my shoulder and jog toward Mrs. Johnson's house. When I get there, my heart is pounding, but I can't tell if it's as much from jogging as it is from wondering what Ellie might have said to Mrs. Johnson. I can't let Mrs. Johnson find out what's going on. She might call the police or something if she finds out that Ellie and I are on our own for too long of a time.

"J.J.!" Ellie squeals and runs toward me. She's been colouring. Markers and sheets of paper are scattered on the table.

"Hi, Ellie! Did you have a good day?"

"Yup. I coloured." She holds up her ink-stained hands for me to see.

"I see that! Can you get your things together now?"

"Hello, dear," Mrs. Johnson says to me. She's about to wipe down the table where Ellie was colouring. "Is your mom working late tonight?"

"Yeah," I reply. *Good. Ellie hasn't said anything.*

Ellie's eyes go wide. "Mom is at work?!" This makes her happy. I can see relief flooding her face. Too bad that I'm lying and she'll soon learn the truth, that nothing has changed. Mom is still lying in that hospital bed.

"Thanks for watching Ellie, Mrs. Johnson."

"No problem, dear." Mrs. Johnson is busy tidying up Ellie's mess, so I pick Ellie up and exit the house quickly.

"Mommy's all better?" Ellie asks as soon as we get outside.

"No, Ellie, I'm sorry. Mom is still in the hospital. But we're going to go and see her right now, okay?" She runs ahead of me toward our front door, anxious to get inside and drop off our things.

I drop my backpack at the front entrance and tell Ellie to go the bathroom. As soon as she's done, I grab our bus passes and we head back out the door. We walk quickly to the bus stop and we wait only a minute or two before the bus pulls up.

When we get to the hospital, my stomach churns at the antiseptic smell that hits me as soon as we walk in. I grab Ellie's hand, holding it a little tighter than usual. My heart pounds as we ride the elevator up to the oncology unit. When the doors of the elevator open, Ellie breaks away from me and sprints toward Mom's room.

Mom is sitting up in her bed, and there is a bit more colour to her face. She looks better than she did last night, and relief washes over me.

"Mommy!" Ellie shrieks. She hops onto the bed and snuggles into her. Despite a string of erupting coughs, Mom lights up at the sight of us.

"How was school?" she asks me.

"Fine."

"Did you go to Mrs. Johnson's house, Ellie?" Mom asks.

"Yeah, but J.J. said you were at work."

I give Mom a pointed look, wondering how we should explain things to Joelle. She knows that I'm lying to Mrs. Johnson. She doesn't understand why we are being secretive.

Mom doesn't miss a beat. "I don't want Mrs. Johnson to worry, so we're going to pretend that I'm at work." Joelle seems satisfied with this, because the hospital is pretty scary to her.

"Mom, I can't find your address book," I say. "I looked everywhere."

"It should be in my drawer."

"It wasn't. Trust me."

"I'm sure that's where I put it. Hmmm," she pauses, clearly trying to backtrack. "You don't need it though."

"What do you mean? I thought we were going to find Dad?"

"Dad?!" Ellie exclaims.

"Shh, never mind, Joelle," I hush her, hoping we can just skip over this part of the conversation. When Joelle was old enough to start asking about who her dad was, Mom would launch into the famous rock star bit and how he needed to travel all the time to perform. I'd bristle at Mom's explanation. Didn't Joelle deserve more? And couldn't we just leave the hero-worshipping behind for this child? It was bad enough that I had gone through it, only to be continually disappointed. Couldn't we spare Joelle the same fate? But Joelle just seemed to accept that response and didn't ask any more questions. Maybe Mom needed to keep saying it so that she could justify to herself why he'd chosen some kind of glamorous life over us, as though it would explain everything.

The only picture Joelle had ever seen of him was one taken on my twelfth birthday. The photo had been tacked on my wall for years, its edges tattered from the number of times I'd reached out to examine it and then tacked it back up. He had a dazzling smile in that photo, and with his shoulder-length hair, his black T-shirt and jeans, and the rings adorning almost every finger, he looked every bit a rock star. To Ellie, I guess it just made sense.

"I know the numbers by heart." Mom's voice is barely a whisper. Her eyes fill with tears, and then she coughs repeatedly before she is able to speak again. I look at her struggling to catch her breath. I can see how crestfallen she is. My heart feels like lead as I process her words. How many times had Mom tried reaching him? I thought it'd been years since she'd last tried, but her face tells me otherwise. Why else would she remember the phone numbers? I see the grief on her face, the years of loneliness. She always believed he'd be coming back, and that one day he'd settle in and stay forever.

"Tell me them, then," I say crisply. I don't want her to hurt any longer. And seeing her like this, realizing what all of these years of waiting for a man who would never come has done to her, I'm livid. I want to shake her and tell her how ridiculous she was to wait. And I want to give him a piece of my mind. I grab the notepad and pen sitting on the side table next to her bed.

I tap the pen impatiently while I wait for the numbers.

"Nobody knows where he is," Mom says.

"Well, we gotta try," I respond with pursed lips. This is no time for excuses, and even Mom knows it.

"Maybe you'll have more luck than I did. Not that it'll mean anything."

"I know what he chose."

Mom looks at me with surprise. "What do you mean?"

"The night he left. I know that you told him he had to make a choice. I was awake that night. I heard it."

"Jayce …" Mom seems startled. If she tries to explain herself, I won't let her.

"Let's have 'em," I say, referring to the numbers. I stare her down, hoping she can feel my frustration.

"You'll need to be prepared that things might not work out the way you hope," Mom says gently.

I smirk. "Are you kidding me? I've spent my whole life feeling that way when it comes to him." And so has she.

"Okay. We'll try to find him." Mom rattles off a series of phone numbers, some from different area codes, and tells me that he's stayed at these places many times over the years. I write them out as carefully as I can so that I'm sure of what I'll be dialing.

"Maybe it'll be different this time …" Her voice trails off as she closes her eyes. I reach for Joelle's hand and tell her it's time to leave. I've got some phoning to do. And I sure hope it will be different this time.

Chapter 5

The phone numbers that Mom gave me turn up nothing. Two of them are disconnected. On the third, a gruff-sounding man answers and hangs up on me before I can explain myself.

"Joe who?" the man bellows.

"Loewen," I respond. He tells me I have the wrong number, and then the line goes dead.

That night there's a knock on the door, and Joelle and I are surprised to see my mom's boss, Lou, and his wife, Freida. They come bearing a box full of food. There is lasagna, a chicken pot pie, a container of soup, two Styrofoam containers of fried chicken and salad, and a plate full of slices of pie from the diner.

"We thought you girls could use this, seeing as your mom is sick right now," Freida explains. My eyes grow wide at the sight of all this delicious food.

"How did you know?" I ask, and Lou tells me that Mom phoned him to let him know what was going on and that she'd be missing more work. I wonder how much Mom has told them.

"You be sure to call on us if you need anything at all, okay?" Freida says. They hand me a piece of paper with a phone number and address. "This is our home address and our phone number. Or you just come right on down to the diner. I mean it. Anything at all."

I thank them profusely. When they leave, Ellie and I dig into the pie slices first. We lick the apple filling that is sticking to our fingers with exaggerated slowness, savouring each bite. It tastes so good, its sweetness dancing on our tongues. For a moment, I forget about not being able to reach my dad.

I decide to call Amanda to ask if I can go with her to her dad's office for Take Your Son/Daughter to Work Day.

"What's up with you, anyhow?" Amanda asks, her voice tinged with annoyance.

"Things are just crazy right now," I say. Instead of pressing further, Amanda launches into a tirade about Luke again and how broken-hearted she is.

"I love him, and I just know he loves me, too," Amanda states. She manages to call him practically every name possible before telling me that she's determined to get him back.

"I'll talk to my dad about Monday, but I'm sure it'll be fine," Amanda says before we hang up, and I'm relieved when we finally say goodbye.

After I put Ellie to bed, I decide to search the house again for the address book. I look in every drawer in every room in the house. I even head back to Mom's room and rummage through her underwear drawer again for good measure, and then every other drawer again, too. I head back to her closet, pull the few items she has hanging in there to the side and toss aside her work shoes and the worn, outdated dress shoes she has lined up on the floor. Nothing. Frustrated, I sit cross-legged on the floor and hold my head in my hands. Mom is counting on me to find Dad, since she can't very well do it while lying in a hospital bed.

It is in this position that I see a wooden panel attached to the side wall of the closet. It is held in place by two small finishing nails. Curious, I tug on the panel with my fingertips. To my surprise, it pops off easily. My eyes grow wide. Inside the wall cavity is a small metal box with a handle, similar to a cash box. I stare at it for a moment before reaching for the handle. It is dusty and cold. The box has a keyhole, but I'm hoping it isn't locked. I turn the metal clasp without difficulty and the box pops open.

Before I look inside, my stomach flips. There's a certain thrill upon stumbling onto something unknown, hidden in the wall. *Who does this belong to? Why is it hidden in the wall? How long has it been here?*

Inside I find worn pieces of paper, folded carefully. They are delicate and soft, I can only imagine the number of times they've been opened and read. My heart beats faster as I pull the items out of the box. There are photos as well. Some are yellowed and stuck together, but I peel them apart carefully.

I gasp at the first image I come upon. It's my mother. There is no mistaking it. She is just a younger version of herself; she has the same big eyes and long hair. She looks to be a teenager in this photo, perhaps my age. She is wearing a pretty blue dress and is standing by a yellow house, her arms in front of her with her fingers laced together. She looks happy and carefree.

Why was Mom hiding these things? And why in a box in the wall? How come I've never seen them before?

I study the other photographs. They must be from her childhood. There is a young girl standing in front of the same yellow house. There is a boy, only slightly taller than the girl, standing beside her. Two adults stand behind them, their hands on the kids' shoulders. I look closer to make sure it's still Mom, but it looks just like her, a miniature version. Are these her parents? And who is this boy? Mom has never mentioned having a brother. Although Mom really hasn't mentioned anything about her family over the years. It's something we're not allowed to talk about.

I turn over the photos and find the years that the photos were taken, written in smeared ink. 1987, 1989, 1992, 1997. The one of her in the blue dress was taken in 1997, and I imagine that it's one of the last photos of her taken by her family. I study the yellow house for any clues as to where it is located. It looks like it's out in the country somewhere, but I can't gather anything beyond that. I see tall spruce trees behind the home and wooden trellises tacked onto the siding.

I gently open one of the letters. The scrawl is messy and hard to read, but a few words in I realize it's a love letter. I scan to the bottom and it is signed "With love, Joe." A love letter from my dad to my mom? I start at the top and read it carefully, savouring every word. Maybe I should feel guilty for going through my mom's private things, but I don't. The letter is proof that my dad really did love my mom, and I need to see this proof. I open the next letter, and the next. Sure enough, all of them are from my dad.

At the bottom of the box, I find an old report card with my mom's name on it. She has perfect grades. I swell with pride reading the words of praise written by her teachers. This discovery makes we wonder what other dreams or goals my mom might have had back then. Did she dream of going to university? Did she have her heart set on a certain career someday?

I see her birth certificate. Born in Meadow Lake, Saskatchewan, on March 18, 1980, to Elsa and Ernie Nichols. Elsa and Ernie. My grandparents. People whose names I've never known until this moment, let alone met. I wonder if this yellow house is in Meadow Lake, if this is where Mom grew up. Could my dad also be from there? Did they meet in Meadow Lake? All I know is that Meadow Lake is north of Saskatoon, the city I've grown up in.

Then I come across one more photo, of Mom and Dad together. They look like they are at a party or in a bar or restaurant. The lighting is dim and there are other people sitting at the tables surrounding them. His arm is draped around her and she is leaning into him. Both of them are smiling wide. They look young, not much older than I am now. On the back is scrawled "Saskatoon, 1997." The year they met. The year before I was born. Mom would have been seventeen years old.

I keep the photos and throw the rest of the contents back into the box and shut the lid. Instead of putting it back into the wall and covering it with the panel, I leave it at the bottom of the closet for easy access. In just a few minutes, I've learned more about my mom's past than what she's told me in sixteen years.

Ellie is fast asleep on the couch, so I drape a blanket on her. I realize how late it is and that tomorrow is Friday, which means that I must have my first journal entry in to Mr. Letts. I decide to call Kurt instead.

He answers on the first ring, and I'm caught off guard because he's answered so quickly. I start stammering.

"J.J., is that you?" he says, chuckling. *Great.* How does he know? Could it only be me since I'm acting like such a blithering idiot?

"Yeah, it's me," I say, laughing back. "Sorry about that."

"No problem. How's your night going?"

"Uh, it's fine," I manage.

"That's what fine sounds like? Yikes."

"Just dealing with a lot right now."

"I get it," he says simply. I hear someone calling for him in the background. "Can you hold on a sec?" he asks.

"Yeah, for sure."

I hear the sound of grunting and heavy breathing for a moment, followed by a high-pitched whimper that sounds like it's coming from a female. What the heck is he doing?

"Sorry, I'm good now," Kurt says, but I'm clearly thrown off and the line goes quiet for several awkward seconds.

"Look, if it's a bad time ..." I feel really uncomfortable now.

"I was just lifting my grandma," Kurt says nonchalantly.

"What?!" I must've heard him wrong.

"I live with my grandma, and she's ill. I take care of her."

"Oh," I reply. I am stunned. "Is she going to be okay?" I think of my mom and how she might never recover. Will Kurt's grandma experience the same fate?

"She had a stroke and has a hard time getting around now. I have to help her get in and out of bed. And I do lots of the cooking and cleaning. She can't use half of her body."

"Whoa," I say, sucking in my breath. "Where are your parents?"

"My grandma's raised me since I was two. I have no idea where my parents are. They are both drug addicts." The way he states it so matter-of-factly, I realize how wrong I've been about him, thinking he's just a slacker who doesn't care about school. "By the way, how is the visit with your grandma going?"

Oh, crap. I forgot about my lie. What do I tell Kurt now? He's been so honest with me and has told me so much already, it feels wrong to keep lying to him.

"Kurt, I know this looks bad, but my grandma isn't actually visiting."

"Uh … okay?" There's no mistaking his confusion.

"My mom is sick and in the hospital and she's all we have," I blurt. "I don't even know my grandma, but it was easier than telling you that I'm alone with my little sister while my mom is fighting for her life."

"That's rough," Kurt says softly. "I'm sorry. Is she going to be okay?"

"That's the thing," I reply, my voice shaking. "I don't think so." And then I break down into tears. They fall hard and fast and I sob into the phone while Kurt listens. Being a teenager and having to be the one in charge of your family is something he understands, and he tells me so.

Chapter 6

Friday morning I hand in my first journal entry to Mr. Letts:

> Life isn't always what you think it's going to be. You grow up thinking you're normal, that you're like every other kid, until you realize one day that you're not. You're not like anyone else around you. And the others just don't get it. They'll never understand you or what you're going through, because they are actually lucky enough to be normal. Meanwhile you struggle and fumble on because you believe there's hope for you and your life. But what if there isn't? What then?

When the bell rings for the morning break, I do a quick walk around the school to look for Kurt, but he's nowhere to be found. I think of our conversation last night. It must be his grandma. He's probably missing school again. Amanda and Danika are whispering to each other and giggling by the entrance. This time, thankfully, they're looking the other direction from me, toward a group of grade twelve guys who are glancing their way. It's awful that I want to avoid them, especially since they are my friends. I mean, Amanda is supposed to be my best friend. Heaven knows, I could sure use one right now.

I decide to head to the hospital. I scurry to the crosswalk at the street and wait at the bus stop. I have to talk to Mom, and I don't want to do it with Ellie around. Sure, I'll miss second and third period, but I'll deal with the phone call home later. After all, it's not like Mom is going to be there to answer the phone.

When I reach the hospital, I enter through the sliding doors and the smells instantly assault me. I hate the smells of sickness, of blood, of antiseptic, and of all things medical. My stomach churns again and I fight the urge to gag. I hear the sounds of monitors beeping and the wheels of stretchers squeaking over the tiled floors. I try not to stare at the patients who are walking around in their hospital gowns, some of them dragging IV poles. I avert my eyes and stare at the ground.

When I get up to Mom's room, she is sitting up and sipping a cup of tea. Despite the shock of seeing her attached to an oxygen tank all of the time now, she looks good, and I feel a wave of hope at the sight of her. Her face lights up when she sees me, and I'm happy I've come. Then she realizes I should be in school, and her face falls a bit.

"Jayce, why are you here?! Is everything okay?"

"Everything's fine, Mom. I had to visit without Ellie. This was the best way."

"But you need to be in school," she admonishes.

"Mom — I've got this. Don't worry about it," I mutter back, though this might not be true. "We need to talk about Dad. And some other things." She stares back at me with her big, beautiful eyes, and I can tell that she knows what I've found.

"I found the box. The one in the wall."

She nods but doesn't say anything.

"I found the pictures, and your birth certificate ..." I don't mention the love letters, because I feel like it'll just hurt her more, though she must know that I've read them. She stays silent and just studies me.

"What about my grandparents, Mom?"

She sighs and folds her hands on her lap, but does not answer.

"Please. It's time I knew more. Especially if we don't find Dad." I know I sound a little whiny, but I'm sixteen years old and there have been a lot of secrets. It's time I hear more of the truth. Mom lies back on the pillow and closes her eyes. She sighs again. I can tell that the wheels are turning in her head — as though she's debating how to continue.

"Please, Mom. It's important."

"I was just a little older than you when I left home," Mom says. "I didn't get along with my parents a lot of the time. They were very strict and had a lot of rules — far more than any other kid I knew. I wasn't allowed to do a lot of things growing up. My parents didn't believe in TV, so I wasn't allowed to watch it. We weren't allowed to join sports teams or school clubs. We weren't even allowed to attend our friends' birthday parties ..."

"What?!" I exclaim. "Why?"

"My dad had been raised in a strict home himself, and he figured that he should raise his kids the same way. We were miserable. We only got to see our friends during school hours. When we left school, it felt like we were going back home to a prison. Dad didn't like doing any activities with us. He wasn't into board games or cards, and when we tried to create our own fun, he got upset at the noise."

"Who is 'we'?" My mind jumps to the boy standing beside Mom in the photograph.

"My brother. Your uncle." Mom's voice shakes with emotion, and she chokes back tears.

"Is he the one in that picture?"

She nods. I don't even have to describe the photo. She knows exactly which one I'm talking about. "His name was John."

"Where is he?"

"As we became teenagers, we wanted to spread our wings. We were tired of living cooped up in our house. We lived on an acreage on the outskirts of town. In Meadow Lake. It was so quiet and boring. John and I talked all the time about how life would be when we could finally leave and move to the city. We started rebelling. My parents tried to tighten the reins even more, but it had the opposite effect." Mom swallows and takes a deep breath. "John was a great kid. So funny and full of life. Everybody loved him." She catches a tear on her cheek with her finger.

"One night, John snuck out of the house to meet up with some friends. They were drinking and speeding down some deserted country roads. The car ended up flipping and two of the four kids died." Mom starts crying openly now. "John was one of them."

I sit on the edge of her bed and touch her shoulder. I can't imagine what it'd be like to lose Ellie.

"John and I had been so close," Mom says. "After he died, everything changed. Our family was never the same. Dad started drinking; Mom would barely get up in the morning. I stopped coming home most days, and, for a while, my mom and dad didn't even seem to notice. Every step back into that house was a reminder of John and what we'd lost. And all of the memories the two of us had from being cooped up in there together."

"So then what happened?" I ask.

"Some girlfriends and I decided to sneak out one night and drive to the city without our parents knowing. My first night there, my girlfriends and I went to this bar to hear some live music. We put on our nicest clothes and did our hair and makeup, hoping we'd be let in, because of course we were too young."

"Did you get in?"

"They let us in just as the band was coming out. And who walked out on that stage but the most handsome man I'd ever seen. He was wearing tight jeans and a black T-shirt, and when our eyes met, he winked at me. I thought I was going to fall over. When the band was done playing, your dad walked right over to me. He said, 'I'm Joe,' and then he invited us out with them. It was like we fell in love instantly."

"I thought my parents wouldn't even know I was gone. I'd gotten away with it so many times by that point, or maybe they'd just stopped caring. But when I went back home with my friends the next morning, I found out my parents had called the police."

"Whoa. Crazy," I say, hanging on to her every word.

"My dad screamed at us when the car pulled up about how worried we'd made our parents, especially because an entire group of teen girls hadn't made it home by morning. 'Are you trying to get yourself killed, too?' he'd yelled. Although I was just trying to have some fun and get away from the grief, I wondered if he was partly right. I'd stopped caring about a lot of things after John died. But the thrill of meeting your dad changed things for me. He was something to be excited about. I had his phone number and I'd call him whenever I had the chance. I had to call him without my parents knowing. Your dad was five years older than me, and my parents would never have approved. Then, a month later, they found out, because the phone bill came and all of our long-distance calls were listed. They nearly hit the roof. By then, I was feeling sick all the time and I'd missed my period. I soon found out I was pregnant."

What?! Mom got pregnant with me that first night with my Dad? This information is shocking to me. My mother, who has always seemed so responsible, so level-headed ... pregnant at seventeen after one night with someone she'd just met? It is almost too much to digest.

Mom catches the shock on my face and laughs. "Nobody is perfect, J.J. And I was lonely after John died. My dad wasn't the greatest father figure. I was desperate for love and attention."

I try to nod my understanding, but it seems so CRAZY.

"And your dad ... well, he was turning into a rock star. In him, I saw a chance at a better life. A chance to leave Meadow Lake and my boring life. A chance to travel the world."

"Did you get pregnant on purpose?" I have to ask. Was I supposed to be her ticket out of there?

"No!" Mom exclaims. "Are you kidding? I was terrified when I found out I was pregnant. Don't get me wrong, I wanted to have you as soon as I found out — there was no doubt about that — but I was only seventeen. It wasn't exactly in the plans." I wait through another coughing fit and hope that Mom will continue the story. It is a part of my life I've never heard, and I'm riveted.

"My dad ordered me out of the house when he found out I was pregnant. And my mom just stood there crying, letting him force me out. I couldn't believe he was willing to cast me aside just because I was pregnant. He told me to never show my face there again — that I'd brought shame to the family. He asked me how I could do this to them, as though it was the worst thing that could have happened to me. I know the circumstances weren't ideal, but I also knew that your dad and I had fallen deeply in love, and I thought I could make it work. Your dad tried talking to them and assuring them that we were really in love, but they hated him at first sight and didn't even give him a chance. I didn't have a lot of choices, so I left for the city."

"And your parents just let you leave? They were serious?" I ask, incredulous. "They'd already lost their son, why would they force away their daughter, too?" I feel a flash of anger toward people I've never met. No wonder she's never talked about them. No wonder the topic has been off-limits.

"They were hurting, I guess," Mom says. But I can see that she doesn't really count this as a viable excuse. "My dad was the boss. We didn't go against him. In all these years I've never spoken to them again." Tears slide in quick succession down her pale cheeks. She looks so tired and worn, and incredibly sad.

I wrap my arms around her and envelop her in a strong hug. She seems so thin and frail, and I want her to feel my love wrapped around her.

"I want you to know that from the moment I found out I was pregnant, I wanted you." Mom looks at me pointedly. "You are the best thing that ever happened to me, J.J. The best gift I could have ever received."

I smile and pull her close again. "Did you go live with Dad, then? Did he want me?"

"We moved into our little place. Dad adored you. He had a special name for you. He made it up on the day you were born."

"Yeah, I know. Jaybird," I say, rolling my eyes.

"He loved you very much, Jayce. He was around unless he was on tour."

"Which was ALL of the time," I point out.

"Things weren't perfect," Mom agrees. "And the past few years … well, I have no answer for that." She's referring to the fact that he left us for good. That Ellie has never even met our father, that he doesn't even know that she exists. That she's been the one to manage everything all on her own. Mom lowers her head and her lips tremble. "I've always tried to do my best by you girls, and yet I know it wasn't quite enough."

"You are amazing, Mom," I tell her, my voice serious. It's like I'm finally realizing how difficult it must've been for her to be away from everything she knew, with a new baby at such a young age, and a boyfriend who was barely around. She always provided for me and then for my sister, as well. She wasn't that much older than I am now, but I can't imagine being in the same position.

"There's something else you need to know," Mom says. "I have some money saved. It's in an envelope, in the cubby where you found the box. There's almost a thousand dollars in there. Take it out and get what you need." Mom's voice falters. I can only imagine the blood, sweat, and tears it must've taken to save that money, and what a big deal it is to use it.

"We need to find him, Jayce." And I know that she's talking about my dad.

"What makes you think he'll even help us?"

"He may not," Mom acknowledges. "But he needs to know about Joelle and what's going on."

"He doesn't deserve it," I mutter. Mom doesn't argue.

"I know. I'll find him," I promise. I don't know how yet, but I'll find him.

Chapter 7

"Any luck?" It's Kurt. He wants to know if I've made any progress in finding my dad.

"No, not yet," I say. "But I did get to talk to my mom about a bunch of stuff."

"I hope I'm not overstepping, but I did some digging," Kurt says slowly.

"What do you mean?"

"I mean, there are thirty-one J. Loewens in Canada. And four of them are in Saskatchewan."

I suck in my breath. *Whoa.*

"I've copied and pasted their numbers and any address information I could find."

Silence.

"Jayce, are you still there?"

"Yeah, I'm here." My voice is barely a whisper. Could one of these numbers be his?

"Look — maybe I went too far. I just thought I could help," Kurt stammers. "I should've minded my own business. I'm sorry, Jayce."

"No, it's good. I'm just surprised." I hadn't managed to copy or print all of the listings I'd found in my last computer search, and Kurt has taken the time to do it for me.

"Can you get away? Bring them here?" I ask.

"Sure thing," he says, and I can sense his relief. "What's your address? I'll be there right away."

When Kurt arrives, he greets Ellie, who is sitting on the couch watching cartoons. She is surprised and excited that we have a new visitor and eagerly chatters away with him. I watch the two of them together and smile. Kurt passes me the list while he's discussing *Max & Ruby* with Ellie. She's delighted that he's interested in the show.

I look down at the paper. Sure enough, Kurt has printed an entire list of Loewens with the first initial *J*. My heart flutters as I scan the listings.

"I hope this is okay," Kurt says shyly.

"Are you kidding? This is great!" I tell him. "I can't believe you did all of this work."

"I just wanted to help somehow, and I know you really need to find your dad quickly."

"I think he's going to be in Toronto or Vancouver or something, if he's still in Canada," I tell him. "At least if he's a successful musician and he tours a lot." Suddenly I feel like I'm twelve years old again, trying to prove that I have a dad but he has an exciting, important job.

Now that I have this list, I should be jumping to the phone, but all I feel is complete and total fear. What if he's not on this list? What if he is? What then? And what do I say?

"Do you want me to try?" Kurt asks. He looks so concerned for me.

I want to be strong enough to do this myself, but I'm just not sure.

"Okay. Go for it," I say. "Just — tell him you're calling because …" I can't think of an excuse.

"Because his daughters need their dad because their mother has a life-threatening illness and is really sick?" Kurt looks at me strangely, as though this should be so obvious.

"I guess," I answer sheepishly. I'm just worried that he's not going to come through for us, and I'm not sure that I can handle that. "Just find out if we have the right person, and we'll go from there."

Kurt starts dialing each number. Time and time again, he thanks the person on the other line and hangs up disappointed. I listen to each call, my heart speeding up with each dialing and then deflating with each hang up. It's an emotional roller coaster — imagining each caller, wondering if it's actually him.

About two-thirds into the list, Kurt's cellphone rings. It's his grandma and she needs him for something.

"Sorry, J.J., I gotta go. But I can help you with this tomorrow," he says. The thought of waiting until tomorrow is excruciating, yet I don't know if I'm ready to do the calls myself.

"That's cool. No problem," I tell him and walk him to the door. "Kurt." I touch his arm and look into his eyes. "Thank you. I mean it." And Kurt flashes me that dazzling smile and heads out the door.

I hover by the door and stare mindlessly out toward the street until Ellie calls for me. I look at her sweet face and her bobbing blond ponytail, and I know what I have to do. I reach for the phone and begin dialing, my heart practically beating through my throat.

By the time I make the eighth phone call, I have started to wonder if my dad doesn't actually exist any longer.

"Hello?" says a man's voice.

"Joe Loewen?" I manage. My hands are sweating so badly I grip the phone tighter, hoping it won't slip from my fingers.

"This is he."

"Joe Michael Loewen?"

"Who is this?"

I have no idea what to say or how to answer. Nothing feels familiar about his voice. But it has to be him. How many Joseph Michael Loewens could there be?

"Hello?" he asks again. "Who is calling?"

There is a long, awkward silence, and then I hang up. I wipe the palms of my hands on my pants and suck in a deep breath. After five years, I have just spoken to my dad. Well, not technically, since I couldn't bring myself to say anything but his name, but it has got to be him.

I call Kurt and tell him that I've found him, that he's one of the Loewens without a listed address.

"What area code?" Kurt asks.

"Three zero six. He's actually in Saskatchewan." The whole notion of this feels like a gigantic kick to the stomach. How could he be so close?

"Give me the number," Kurt says. I repeat it back to him, and in a few seconds he tells me that the prefix of the phone number coincides with the city of Prince Albert. I practically choke. Prince Albert? It's only an hour and a half from Saskatoon; 142 kilometres away.

"No," I say. "It can't be." I can barely breathe.

"This can't be right," I say again.

"Maybe it's just his home base and you've caught him in between tours," Kurt offers. But as soon as he says it, we both know it sounds ridiculous.

"How could he live so close to us all of this time?" I ask feebly, tears threatening to burst from my eyes. "He couldn't come and see us even once? Not a visit? Not a phone call? It's been *years*!" My voice gets louder with each word. "And Ellie — he doesn't even know she exists!" I hear Kurt gasp.

"I don't know what to say, J.J. But you have to talk to him. Find out what the deal is."

"I know," I say. Our conversation peters out. I'm too preoccupied with what I've learned.

Although my mind is spinning a mile a minute, I know what I have to do. I have to get us to Prince Albert.

Chapter 8

It's Monday morning and I'm making a phone call that is about to change everything.

"Joe Loewen? Why, yes, my dear. He just lives up the street from us. Been there for about ten years now, I'd say. He tends to keep to himself, that one. But he does come to our parties. Now, why were you asking, again, dear?" The dear woman clucks. She is Marj Wilson. Her voice sounds gentle and kind.

"Uh, he's an old friend. Just wanted to make sure he was still living in town," I stammer. My heart is beating so wildly, it takes my breath away. "Thank you for your help!" I blurt, hanging up before she can say anything else. It feels rude to hang up on the nice woman, but what else can I say to her? The phone is slippery in my sweaty hands. Could this really be him? Could I have found him?

Kurt had called early this morning and offered me a ride to school. When he got to the house, we'd googled

"Joe Loewen Prince Albert Saskatchewan" on Kurt's cell-phone, and we'd found a photo of a man who looked like my dad in a random blog post. These people named Marj and Marcel Wilson like to post photos of their travels, their family get-togethers, and the semi-annual parties they host for their neighbours. The man who looked like Dad was holding a beer and smiling into the camera. His hair was cropped short and his fingers were free of any of the rings I remembered him wearing, but the black T-shirt he was wearing and his eyes and his smile were enough to assure me it was him. Sure enough, Dad's name appeared below the photo. Kurt and I had scrolled through more photos, looking for anything else that might have been important, but we only came upon the one photo. We'd looked up Marj and Marcel Wilson on Canada 411 and I'd scribbled down their address and phone number.

After I hang up on Marj, I realize that I should have asked her what Dad's actual house number is. I can't go door to door, as that would arouse too much suspicion. And what is the alternative? Hide in some bushes, watching people leave their homes, hoping I'll finally spot him? No, I need to know which house he lives in first.

Should I call back? I've already hung up on the poor woman. What if I made her angry and she doesn't want to help me now? I have to take the chance. I fumble with the numbers on the phone. I almost jump when I hear the first ring.

"Hello?" the same kind voice answers.

"Hi. I know I just called and I'm sorry to bother you, it's just that I'm planning a visit sometime soon and it's been so long, and I can't really remember which house Joe lives in …"

"Oh, 105 Mitchellson. Is that right, Marcel — Joe lives at 105?" Her voice trails off, as though she's covered the phone.

"Who are you talking to?" a man's voice says, irritated. "You shouldn't be giving people's information over the phone like that." I can tell he's suspicious already. I feel flooded with fear.

"Thank you, ma'am. That's all I needed. Take care," I say, ending the conversation again.

Mitchellson Road. After all this time, I know where he lives. I'll pack some things, we'll take the bus to Prince Albert, and Dad will take care of us.

I call Mom to tell her we are going. She wants me to talk to him on the phone first instead of travelling all the way there alone, but I think he needs to see us face to face to make this real for him. This is practically life or death, and he's had too much time away from us to allow him this distance now.

I hang up the phone with Mom and look at Kurt.

"I'm proud of you," he says, squeezing my hand. "This takes guts." I feel so grateful for him and all that he's done for me, how he's become such a great support to me.

"You're not taking the bus, Jayce."

"Yes, Kurt, we are."

"I will drive you guys. You need someone with you for this. You aren't just showing up at some house in a strange city."

"What about school?" I say, but Kurt just smirks.

"I think we both know I can manage that." Although Kurt's missed so much school caring for his grandma, he seems to be able to keep up with his schoolwork just fine.

"Okay," I agree. I won't put up a fight on this, and Kurt knows it.

We're heading somewhere we've never been before. I have to make sure that Ellie is safe and well taken care of, and if Dad doesn't come through, what then? The thought of having Kurt with us makes me feel so much better.

"Ellie, we're going on a big adventure, so we need to pack some stuff."

"I don't wanna go," Joelle whines.

"Sure you do. It'll be so much fun." I am rolling up sweaters for the two of us and stuffing them in a backpack. I've got some snacks to take with us, courtesy of Mom's secret stash of money. I was able to buy some essentials for us, but I couldn't bring myself to buy more than that for now. Who knows what the future will bring and how long Mom will be in the hospital. We're going to need that money for a million other things, too.

I'm not going to bring a lot with us; we're going to find Dad, we'll let him know what's going on, and hopefully he'll come back with us right away. I don't want to leave Mom alone for any longer than I have to.

"I wanna stay HERE." Joelle's bottom lip is sticking out and her arms are crossed. She's watching me, uncertain that this adventure will actually be any fun.

"We're going to find Dad," I say, finally, and Joelle jumps at me excitedly.

"We're going to see Daddy?" she shrieks. I see how desperate she is to meet him and make him real to her, and it breaks my heart. Mom and I have tried not to talk about him much, but that doesn't stop a kid from wanting a dad. Joelle doesn't even realize that it's weird that she's never met him.

I check the cash in my wallet again. I don't want to lose what my mom has worked so hard to save. I'm starting to realize just how much is riding on my dad taking us in. Food. Shelter. Survival.

I struggle with what we'll do if things don't work out, but I can't let my mind go there just yet.

To my surprise, Ellie and I fall asleep on the way there. As Kurt pulls up to a stop sign at the highway junction just outside of Prince Albert, we both wake up, groggy and disoriented. It is grey and dreary outside, and, instead of feeling excited, I feel that my mood is matching the day. Ellie whines for a snack, and I fumble for a granola bar in my backpack. I can't think about eating. My stomach is in knots, and at times I'm so queasy I might be sick.

I type Mitchellson Road into Google Maps on Kurt's phone. Ellie is chattering endlessly about random things, but I'm barely paying attention. The closer we get to my dad, the worse my stomach feels. It takes about ten minutes for us to find Mitchellson Road. Kurt pulls over when we reach the corner leading into the crescent. By this time, I'm trembling almost uncontrollably. It's all I can do not to run away. Ellie is still oblivious and seems completely relaxed. How I wish I was her — so trusting, so sure that everything is fine. My mind catalogues the metal garbage bin near the bus stop; at least if I get sick, I can do it in there instead of spraying it all over the street.

"Okay, Ellie, let's go," I announce.

"I can pull up right to the house," Kurt says, but I shake my head.

"No, stay here and wait," I instruct him. He squeezes my hand and nods.

"I'll be right here," he assures me. Even he looks nervous enough to be sick.

I step out onto the sidewalk and open Ellie's door. She looks around and sees that we aren't in front of anyone's house yet.

"How much farther?" Ellie asks, and I realize that, for a four-year-old, this has already been a long morning.

"We're almost there, Ellie." I kneel down in front of her so that we can be eye to eye, my knees balancing on the rough sidewalk. "Look, Ellie. Dad doesn't know we're coming," I start. "He is going to be very surprised."

Ellie claps her hands in anticipation. "A surprise!" she says, excitedly.

"Yeah, but we might not be staying with him. We have to tell him about Mom, that she's sick. We're going to ask him for help," I try to explain.

Ellie looks confused, but takes my hand and pulls me up. We make our way down the street.

My legs feel like they're made of lead, and they seem to get heavier with each step I take. I feel as though I'm practically dragging myself forward. I study the homes. This is a picturesque neighbourhood. The houses are all variations of the same soft colours. The yards are well manicured. Basketball nets are tacked onto many of the attached garages, and hockey nets line the sides of many driveways. This is clearly a family-friendly neighbourhood, and it's much newer and nicer than where I've grown up.

Slowly we pass each house and I scan house numbers ... 3, 39, 47, 79, 95 ... Marj and Marcel Wilson's house is number 95; it is practically a botanical garden, with all of the flowers planted in the yard. There's a garden gnome almost every two feet. I walk a little faster past their house, out of nerves and the sense that I've endangered us already by phoning them twice and fishing for information.

And then I see it: 105. A light-blue two-storey house. It's pretty modest and simple — certainly not the house I'd envision a successful musician to have. The reality of this is like another sucker punch to the gut. It is neat and tidy from the outside, though sparsely planted compared to the Wilsons' yard. There is a welcome mat on the front step. The driveway is empty, but the car could be parked inside the attached garage. There is little on the outside of this house that would tip me off as to whether or not this house actually belongs to my dad.

My heart hammers in my chest. I crouch behind a hedge with Ellie just before his house, just so I can gather myself and figure out what to do. I've never been so scared in my life. Ellie is looking up at me with some apprehension. I have to do this. For me and for her. For Mom.

"Let's go," I say with more conviction than I feel. My knees are practically knocking together and I hope that my legs won't give out altogether.

We walk up the driveway and the world starts spinning for me. That's it. I know I'm going to pass out. He'll open the door and see that some strange girl has fainted on his driveway and wonder what the heck is going on. I bet he won't even recognize that it's his own daughter.

Ellie breaks away from me and sprints to the doorway to ring the doorbell before I can do anything.

"No!" I croak, but it's too late and the chime of the doorbell echoes to the outside.

We stand side by side. Sweat glides down my temples. I can feel my shirt sticking to my back. We wait for what feels like forever.

"I guess he's not here," I say, ready to turn around. And then we hear the shuffling of steps, and through the glass in the door we see a shadow approaching. I stop breathing for a moment, until a pretty, brown-haired woman of about forty swings open the door. She's dressed in capris and a T-shirt and is barefoot. Her face looks kind. She has large brown eyes with thick lashes and wears very little makeup. A tea towel is draped over her shoulder. She peers at us curiously.

"Are you looking for Maddie?" she wonders. "She's at preschool right now. I'm just about to go and get her for lunch." She is talking directly to Ellie, who must be around the same age as Maddie.

"Uh … no," I struggle to answer. My heart fills with relief. We've got the wrong house. Clearly Joe Loewen doesn't live here because there's a nice little family here. Maddie lives here and she's in preschool.

"We have the wrong house," I state matter-of-factly. The woman looks closer at us and leans into the doorway. She's clearly curious.

"Can I help you with what you're looking for?" she asks. Ellie is about to tell her what we're doing and I quickly talk over her.

"Oh! I got the numbers mixed up. It's 501 we need, not 105. I don't know how I got that mixed up!" I laugh nervously. I don't even know if there is a 501, and maybe this woman knows 501 doesn't exist. Maybe she'll call me on it.

"Okay," the woman says hesitantly.

"Thank you!" I say quickly. "Let's go, Ellie." I take her by the hand and we turn back down toward the driveway. The woman remains standing at her doorway watching us, until I realize that a car is pulling into the driveway at the same time as we are leaving, and she's probably waiting for whoever is pulling up. It's a simple black four-door sedan. The door swings open and a tall, slim man steps out.

He smiles at us politely. My heart literally stops. It's him. He's wearing beige dress pants and a button-up shirt — certainly not rock star clothing. It's been so long, but I'd recognize his features anywhere. My eyes remain fixated on him. He continues toward us to get to his front door, but then does a double take as he passes me.

I see the blood drain from his face, and I know that he's recognized me. I stand absolutely still, gazing at him.

He looks good. There is some grey that peppers his brown hair, and there's no question he looks older. He even has really pronounced crow's feet at his eyes, something I don't really remember on his face when I was twelve. But what is he doing here?

"Joe?" the woman calls out. She is wringing the tea towel in her hands uncertainly.

My dad is oblivious to her in this moment. He stares at me intently, but looks as though he's seen a ghost.

I stare back at him, flooded with tons of emotions. I'm angry, sad, relieved — a million things at once. We both remain there, our eyes locked together for what feels like forever.

"Joe?!" The woman's voice is a bit higher this time.

We take each other in, silently, until Ellie tugs on my arm.

"J.J.," she whispers. I lean down to scoop her up and look our dad straight in the eyes. It's now or never.

"Yes, Dad. It's me. Jayce. And this is your daughter Joelle."

Chapter 9

The woman, Dad's wife, is named Mallory. She is weeping openly into the tea towel now. We are seated awkwardly around their dining table, in their cute-as-a-button home. Dad will barely look at me now, instead preferring to study Ellie, this foreign, near-perfect specimen that he's just learned is his. He is tugging at his hair with his fists; tears pour down his cheeks and pool onto the table in messy splatters.

"You can't be serious," Mallory says, though she knows deep down that this is real. "How?" she says aloud. There is pain and confusion in her eyes as she takes this all in. I get that this is a lot to take in. And yet, I want to say the exact same thing. Ellie and I have been sitting quietly while this unfolds.

"Mallory, I …" Dad struggles for an explanation but closes his mouth.

"*You have daughters with someone else?*" Her voice is sharp. This echoes what I want to say to him. *You are married and have kids with someone else?*

"I had Jayce a long time ago — years before I met you," he stammers. "This other one — I had no idea about."

"Her name is Joelle," I state angrily. "She's four years old. She's not some random kid. She's Joelle Marie Loewen, born April 7, 2011. And you're her dad."

"Oh my God," Mallory holds her head in her hands, sobbing. "The same age as Maddie!"

"I was touring … it was wrong."

"You haven't toured in eight bloody years, Joe."

These words pummel me deep within. Eight years? All these years of us thinking he was living his dream, touring with his band. The math doesn't add up.

"You didn't choose the band?" What was he leaving us for? I can barely breathe. Both Mallory and Dad look puzzled, but I'm the one who is confused.

"What do you mean?" I ask. "You're not a musician?"

Dad shifts uncomfortably in his seat. "Of course. Well, I was … it's been a long time."

"Apparently!" I choke, and my voice is one I don't even recognize. This explains why I haven't been able to find anything remotely current about Raven's Spell.

"You acted like the perfect dad whenever you came around. And all this time it was a big lie? You weren't touring? You were leading a double life with her?!" I'm hysterical now. "What about Mom? You lied to her all this time, too? She *loved* you! She waited for you for years so that we could be a family …" My body is wracked with sobs, and Ellie starts crying, too. She rubs my back and snuggles into me. How is it that she's comforting me? I should be protecting her from all of this. From this man who is nothing like she's been told.

Mallory stands and throws her arms in the air as though she's had all she can hear.

"Mal, no, don't go," Dad says pathetically.

"I have to. I have to pick up Maddie. Your other daughter, remember?" she replies icily.

"You shouldn't be driving like this," he reasons. "I'll go get her."

"Ha," Mallory spits. She looks at Ellie and me, as though being alone with the two of us right now would be too much. She wipes mascara from her bottom eyelids and straightens up. The door clicks behind her and she's gone.

We're left alone. I wish Ellie wasn't here. I wish I could shield her from this. I sit there, staring at his face. He looks terrible, panicked even. It's so quiet I can hear a clock ticking in between his sniffles.

"Jayce," he starts, and then swallows. "I never meant for all of this. It's not quite what you think."

"What do you mean?! You have a whole other family — and you've been lying to us both!"

"I loved your mother. I always have. I've never stopped."

"Riiigghhhtt …" I manage. "Because that's love. Leaving her to raise us alone all these years, only showing up when you wanted a booty call."

"Jayce!" Dad interjects.

"What? What else would you call it? You'd stay for a couple of days here and there and then be on your merry way. And all that time we thought you were touring — that you might be someone special." The last part is dripping with sarcasm. "And it turns out, you weren't some successful rock star — you were a lying, cheating, married man! I wanted to believe it all. I wanted to believe that you weren't around because of the music. Being a musician doesn't make it okay to abandon your family, either, but at least telling people my dad was on tour made for a cool story. But the truth is you're nobody." I hug Ellie close as she cries beside me. I wish she wasn't here to hear this, but I'm not done yet.

"My mom has loved you since day one. She has worked so hard to raise us without you, and this is what she gets? She doesn't deserve this. Did she know about all of this?" I wave my hand around the room. My eyes scan the house as I do it. Happy family photos line the walls; cheery floral throw cushions adorn the couch. It's bright and airy and beautiful.

He hangs his head in shame and shakes his head no.

"How could you do this to her? To us?" Ellie has curled up into my lap now and is resting her head on my shoulder.

"Jayce, I've loved your mother since the day I met her. I swear," he says.

"This isn't love. It's deceit. Abuse. Lies. It's all fake."

"It was so great in the beginning — she and I. And you came along. It was so good. I really did start touring all the time then," he explains. "I got caught up in the lifestyle and the partying, and I just couldn't bring myself to come home and be the family man I knew you guys needed." I look at him with contempt. He has tears and snot running together in streams down his face. He looks pathetic.

"Do you know what we went through? All the years you were gone? All the times you'd show up for a while, how excited we'd be and how scared, because we never knew when you'd take off again?"

He cries even more at my words.

"Remember my twelfth birthday? When you stayed as long as you did? How Mom said you had to make a decision. I know all about the choice you made. That's when Mom got pregnant with Joelle. She kept trying to get a hold of you, but you'd disappeared off the face of the earth. And you missed all of this ..." I look down at Ellie. He looks at her and sobs even harder. How could he do this to this innocent little child?

"I had no idea," he manages through his tears.

"No, you wouldn't. Because by then you had a baby on the way, didn't you?"

He nods solemnly. "I decided after that visit that it would be best to leave you for good. I knew I couldn't be the person you both deserved. I was with Mallory already, and I was getting a fresh start when I found out she was pregnant. I decided I'd be the best father I could be to our child."

"At least you showed up for *somebody*."

The room goes quiet again except for the sound of his crying. I'm surprisingly dry-eyed now; I feel anger more than anything.

"I've obviously come looking for you for a reason," I say, my eyes full of disgust. I don't know how I ever thought he'd be able to help. He probably won't care at all about our situation. "We need help. Mom is sick."

I watch his eyes light up with concern.

"It's lung cancer. Stage four." I don't want to mention that she could be dying alone right now while I'm here with Ellie beside me.

"What do you need?" he asks quickly. "Money? A place to stay? Anything …"

I look at this man, who thinks that perhaps he can fix everything in one quick swoop.

I shake my head in disgust and stand from the table. I take Ellie by the hand and head toward the door. He stays seated at the table, his face bereft.

"A father," I say clearly. "We need a father."

I pull Ellie outside with me and the cool air feels welcome on our tired, tear-stained faces.

I rush her down the driveway and up the street, back to Kurt's waiting car. Curiosity gets the best of me and I glance back once, to see if he's run after us, if he's following somewhere behind. But the sidewalk is empty.

It figures. I don't know why I'd have hoped for anything else.

Chapter 10

When we get back to the car, Kurt is standing by the passenger door, holding his arms out to me as I approach. When I step into them, fresh tears find their way.

"It was awful," I whisper to him. He squeezes Ellie and me and then opens the doors for us. He looks as though he might cry as he drives. He stops at a drive-through and orders food for us. I thank him and try to nibble at my food, but it is tasteless. Ellie gobbles hers, and I'm grateful that she's eating.

"Do you want to talk about it?" Kurt asks me, finally, and I do, but I can't find the words. Not until we're almost back in Saskatoon. Until then we drive in silence, with the radio as distraction. I can't believe what I've just learned. Of all of the scenarios I imagined, this was not one of them. Kurt can't believe it either, and he doesn't know what to say the whole ride home.

"Do you want to go home or to see your mom?" he asks gently, as we head back into the city. I don't know that I'm ready to talk to Mom yet, and I feel so drained. He drives us home. Kurt stays with us, and his presence is calming and soothing to me. I relay everything to him, and he lets out a long whistle at the end of it.

Then the phone rings. It is Amanda.

"There you are! I've been trying you like a million times already today." She sounds angry.

"Well, I'm here now," I say with impatience.

"Thanks a lot, you know," she says coolly. "You stood us up."

"Stood you up for what?" I have no idea what she's talking about.

"You asked to come with us to my dad's work. We waited outside your house. My dad was *late* because of you."

I groan inwardly. Take Your Son/Daughter to Work Day. *Ugh. How could I have forgotten?*

"I'm so sorry, Amanda — it completely slipped my mind."

"What do you mean, it *slipped your mind*? It's school, for crying out loud."

"I know — it's just — I was out of town." I'm stammering. Maybe this is the time I tell her what's really happening. Surely she'll understand when she hears what I'm dealing with.

"You've been acting so strangely lately, and you barely talk to me. You know how much I'm going through with Luke and everything, and you just don't seem to care. I thought we were closer than that. Then you ditch me today and tick off my dad. I mean, what could I tell him? 'I have no idea where she is, Dad. She was supposed to be here.'"

"I'll apologize to your dad — I will. I didn't mean for this to happen …"

"Look, J.J., I'm done. Honestly. I thought you were a better friend than this." And with that she hangs up and I'm left with a dial tone.

I look stricken when I hang up the phone.

"What now?" Kurt asks. "Your face says it all."

"Well, my best friend has pretty much called off our friendship. I messed up. I bailed on Take Your Son/Daughter to Work Day. I was going to work at her dad's firm. That and she doesn't feel like I'm there for her anymore."

"What?!" Kurt says, shocked. "Does she know what's going on for you right now?"

"I haven't told her. I haven't really made it that far."

"Maybe you should talk to her then."

"That's the thing. I don't even know what I want anymore. I'm so confused. I'm really starting to question whether she would be able to handle this or not."

Kurt pulls me in for another hug, and I practically melt. His hugs are so strong and warm, and they make me feel safe.

"You've been really amazing, Kurt," I tell him. We sit on the couch together for a long time before he tells me he has to go. I walk him to the door and just as he is about to step out, he turns and plants a sweet and soft kiss on my cheek. My insides go warm. I blush and smile and wave goodbye.

I shut the door and take inventory of my day. I've managed to skip out of a big obligation, travel to another city, find my dad, possibly break up a family, and lose my best friend, all in about twelve hours. Kurt's hugs and his kiss are the definite highlights, but they don't come close to erasing the nightmare of this day.

Chapter 11

"Mom, this is my friend Kurt." Kurt holds out his hand and Mom shakes it tentatively. She gives him a polite smile and then shifts uncomfortably on her bed. She gives me a pointed look, and I know she's wondering what is going on. And I think she's worried about me having a new guy friend.

Ellie jumps onto Mom's bed and snuggles into her happily. Mom visibly relaxes at having Ellie close to her.

"Kurt's been helping me with things," I say.

"What kinds of things?" Mom says, a bit sharply.

"He researched all of the Loewens in Canada so that we could narrow down the search. He's basically the reason we found Dad." I feel sick at the thought of telling her what I've learned.

"Did you find him?" Mom's voice is small and childlike.

"Yes," I start, sucking in my breath. She is searching my face for clues, hoping she'll like the news.

I don't want to relive this with Ellie around. "Kurt, could you take Ellie for a walk?" I ask.

"You bet," Kurt replies, and Ellie jumps off the bed, eager to spend time with Kurt. Mom's eyes follow them out. She seems worried about letting Ellie walk off with Kurt, who is a complete stranger to her.

"He's fine, Mom," I assure her. "She's in good hands."

Mom nods and decides to trust me. She's far more interested in hearing about my dad.

"We went to his house in P.A." I start wringing my hands. I'm fidgety all over. How do I start this? A detailed play-by-play of what happened? With Mallory first?

I want to be strong and act like none of this matters. I want to be brave for Mom, but instead my voice wavers and tears prick my eyelids before I can say anything else. I want to tell her everything in a way that makes it seem as though I could care less, so that she isn't disappointed or hurt. She's defended him all these years, and her reward is to experience the pain of him choosing to leave us for good. And then I think of him married to Mallory, in a perfect house in a perfect neighbourhood with another daughter that he adores and spends each day with. My stomach churns uncontrollably again and I fight the urge to vomit.

She is looking at me expectantly. Although he has caused her this pain, I see that in some way he still holds the key to her heart; there's no mistaking it. Not knowing how to continue in a way that will make this easier, I blurt: "He's married, Mom. For *years*. To a woman named Mallory. And they have a four-year-old daughter

— same age as Ellie." I'm practically panting from letting the words tumble out of me.

Mom stares at me vacantly. It is dead silent except for the hum of the oxygen compressor. I stare back, waiting for a flicker of emotion from her, but she sits stunned. She blinks. And then blinks again. The silence is deafening. I can't handle her reaction — how subdued it is, how unemotional it seems. She sits, unmoving. I wonder if maybe she hasn't heard me.

"Jayce," Mom says weakly. Her voice is so quiet and shaky, I decide something else is wrong.

"I'll get help, Mom …" I respond quickly. Should I press the call button or run into the hallway and flag someone down? I decide on heading to the hallway and turn to leave.

"No," Mom croaks. I spin around, surprised.

"Are you sure?" I ask.

She nods and lays her head back onto her pillow.

"Mom?!" I'm so worried. She looks as though she might pass out. "Are you okay? What should I do?"

Mom waves at me as if to say not to worry, but her ashen face and her downcast eyes tell me a different story.

"He knows about Ellie?" Mom says finally. Her voice is nothing more than a whisper.

"He knows."

She nods but her eyes remain blank.

"Mom, his wife had no idea. We were a total surprise to her. She left to go and pick up their daughter from preschool, but she was super upset …" I don't know what else to say. I'm practically slicing my mother's heart with a butcher knife right now. "He tried to tell me that he loved us, that he'd never stopped. Then he said he felt so guilty about being gone so much that Mallory and his other daughter were his chance to start over and do things right." I scoff at my own words. They sound ridiculous. "How could he have a completely different life?" I ask her, my voice steadily rising. "How could he just forget about us and play the perfect family man with them?" Tears spring down my cheeks yet again.

"What about his music?" I barely make out Mom's words, she's so quiet.

"Apparently he quit music a long time ago. Guess that career didn't really pan out after all," I spit. My fingers curl into fists at my words. I can feel my whole body tense. "Whatever stories he told you, they were all lies," I say.

Mom's breathing becomes more laboured. I see that I've stressed her out far too much.

"We don't need him, Mom," I cry, rushing to her to wrap my arms around her. We cling to each other, our bodies shaking uncontrollably, wracking with sobs. I'm relieved that she is finally showing emotion, but scared of how badly my news has hurt her.

Her thin, frail body feels so delicate in my arms, and I feel another surge of anger at how unfair this is to her. Part of me debates telling her about how he tried to convince me of his love for my mom, how he swore that he'd never stopped loving her, but I can't bring myself to do it. The words mean nothing now, and I don't want to give her false hope. He's not coming back to us. Not now. Not ever. I can't protect her from this horrible truth.

"Jayce." Mom seems so heartbroken, so spent. "It's time."

"Time for what?" I have no idea what she means. Her eyes are closed now, and she is leaning back onto her pillow. She seems to be trying to gather her thoughts. I wait for what feels like an eternity for her to speak again, and, when she does, her words are crystal clear.

"It's time to call your grandparents."

Chapter 12

When I show up for school on Tuesday, Mr. Letts eyes me carefully.

"I hear you didn't attend our work day," he says.

How would he know that? Then I see Amanda, in the back corner, glowering at me with her arms crossed. Mystery solved. Amanda's ratted on me for sure.

"I had to go out of town," I say. "Can I write an essay or something in place of the work day?"

Mr. Letts swallows and turns back to his desk. He picks up my blue notebook, the new journal with my first entry.

"About your writing," Mr. Letts continues, handing me the book. "I'm wondering if there isn't more we should be talking about."

Please don't talk about what I wrote. Why did I write it, anyway? Why couldn't I write about nice things like puppies and butterflies and a perfect life? Why must I write about things that make teachers and adults suspicious?

"Everything is fine, really, Mr. Letts. I was just in a really bad mood when I wrote it." I smile brightly and take the book from him. "Everyone has a bad day now and then," I add.

He nods and smiles, but he seems genuinely concerned. He pauses before turning back to his desk, and I sigh with relief when he decides to start class.

I glance back at Amanda and she shoots me another dirty look. I guess she really is done with our friendship after all.

Kurt and I have lunch together under a tree outside of the school. We are quiet, and focused on our sandwiches, but it's a comfortable silence. Amanda, Danika, and Jenna pass us as they cross the schoolyard. They ignore me, even though there's no way they haven't seen me sitting there.

"Yikes," Kurt mutters under his breath. He shakes his head.

"It's fine," I say, but what I really want to do is cry. Life seems to be getting lonelier by the second.

"A true friend would be there for you," Kurt points out. In all fairness, though, I haven't even mentioned what's going on in my life to Amanda. "And you shouldn't have to worry about whether or not they can handle it," he adds. "Someone is either a good friend or they're not."

"My mom wants me to call my grandparents," I say, changing the subject.

"Are you going to?"

"I guess so. I mean, what choice do I have? And if Mom thinks it's time … it's just … she hasn't talked to them in almost two decades. And they've never even tried to contact her." I chew at the skin on my lip. "What kinds of people go that long without trying to find their daughter? And grandchild? They knew she was going to have a baby. How could you refuse a baby? I mean, look at my dad. He didn't look for us, either, and look what kind of a person he turned out to be."

Kurt nods. He pulls the crust off his sandwich and pops it into his mouth.

"And what do we say? 'Remember how you couldn't handle having a grandchild then, well, here's two grand-children, now. And, by the way, all those years you lost with your daughter, you can't make that up. Now she's dying.'" My voice breaks on the last words and I turn into another puddle of tears. How many tears can one person cry?

Kurt rubs my shoulder and hands me his napkin. I take it and wipe my cheeks.

"Does this really have a chance of working?" I ask, even though I don't really expect an answer.

"They've been lost to you already, so, technically, you have nothing to lose," he offers.

I want to believe that is true, but I'm not sure that I can handle any more rejection. If Mom dies and my dad can't care for us and my grandparents refuse to — what then? I suppose I will take care of both Ellie and myself. The thought is terrifying, but it might be all I have.

"You're a really strong person, Jayce," Kurt tells me. "If they can't see what a special person you are, then they don't deserve you, anyway."

I smile weakly and thank him. After alienating my best friend and getting rejected by my dad, it feels great to have someone in my corner.

When Ellie and I get to the hospital that night, we get the shock of our lives. First of all, when we get to Mom's room, her bed is empty. It has been stripped of all its bedding, and we're greeted by a plastic mattress. I immediately panic and rush out of the room, demanding to know where she is. My heart is thumping so wildly, I feel like I might faint.

"Your mom has been transferred over to the Palliative Care Unit," the nurse at the desk tells me. "She's up on the fifth floor." I breathe a sigh of relief, but still feel uneasy.

"What is palliative care?" I ask. I'm not sure I want the answer.

The nurse looks startled. She looks back and forth between me and Joelle. She's not sure whether or not to continue.

"It's … it's for patients who require … patients who have life-threatening illnesses … patients are given comfort and care as they transition …" She stumbles on her words.

I nod, because she doesn't need to say more, especially since Ellie is standing beside me, her huge blue eyes fixated on the nurse. I get it. She's dying. They know it, and they're trying to help her live her last days.

I want to scream and punch something, or take that stupid hospital cart that's filled with medical supplies and shove it down the hallway. I imagine the contents being catapulted all over the hallway, the clanking of the metal bowls as they bounce off the floors. I picture myself taking the brakes off Mom's stretcher and wheeling her out of there as fast as I can. I wheel her right out the doors, down the sidewalk, and all the way to the river. She's smiling and excited, asking me to go faster, as Ellie and I hoot and holler and skip. We go toward the riverbank, where towering trees and lush green shrubs await. I find us a secret hollow down by the river's edge, and Mom tears off her oxygen mask, miraculously able to breathe effortlessly again. She gets up and dances, full of energy. She grabs us girls by the hands and spins us around.

"Thank you for saving me," she says, kissing us on our foreheads. We twirl around, the hot sun warming our faces and filling us with hope. We giggle and fall onto our backs on the soft, mossy ground and stare up at the billowy clouds.

I blink, and instead of seeing clouds I find myself staring at the hospital's grey ceiling tiles and an unforgiving fluorescent light. Ellie is pulling on my arm and calling my name.

I come out of my daydream and we make our way to the elevator.

The second shock of our lives comes when we find Mom's new room. We hear soft voices as we approach. I grip Ellie's hand a little too tightly, and I realize how nervous and scared I am. We turn the corner and see a woman in her sixties sitting on the edge of the bed, obstructing my view of Mom. At first I think I must've led us into the wrong room. I turn on my heels to leave, but something stops me in my tracks. I glance back at the figure on the bed. Her head is bowed, and she is holding the patient's hand. I hear soft sobs from the two of them. The room feels heavy with emotion. Even though I think I'm violating someone's poignant moment, I can't seem to budge.

A doctor enters the room and smiles warmly at us.

"Hello," she says. She's about Mom's age and looks strangely like her.

"Hi," Ellie and I say in unison, our voices quiet and curious.

At the sound of our voices, the figure on the bed swivels around and we hear Mom's voice.

"Girls," she says hoarsely.

The woman on the bed smiles at us, but she's looking at us cautiously. Her eyes travel between the two of us as though she's studying us.

"I'm Doctor Maniah," the pretty doctor continues. She's holding a clipboard in one hand, and she holds out her other hand for us to shake, which Ellie and I both do. "I'll be looking after your mom," she says. She steps closer to the bed and then writes down the numbers she sees on the medical equipment. We watch her adjust the oxygen tube on Mom's face, and then she pats Joelle on the head before saying goodbye and leaving the room.

I look at the woman on Mom's bed. She is short and fairly round. Her blond hair is tinged with grey, and it is cropped close to her head in soft curls. She wears glasses. When I look at her more closely, I see that she has big blue eyes.

The eyes. They look familiar, but I can't think why. Mom sees the confusion on my face.

"Jayce and Ellie, this is your grandma," Mom says simply.

My eyes feel as though they are going to pop out of my head. This is her mother? My grandma? How did she get here? And why is she sitting on my mom's bed holding her hand? Why is Mom letting her into our lives? I know she said it was time to call them, but I just wasn't expecting this so soon, and I'm not sure I like this woman being here.

"Hello," the woman says gently. She smiles at us but I bristle at her. I hold Ellie close beside me.

"Come here," Mom says, patting the bed. I stay firmly planted where I am, but Ellie runs toward Mom immediately and snuggles into her on the bed. This woman, who is apparently my grandma, looks at Ellie and wipes a tear from her eye.

"She's beautiful," she tells my mom, and my mom has to wipe away her own tears at her mother's words.

Ellie gives the woman a big, toothy grin and starts chattering to her, even asking her for a high-five. I stand statue-like, trying to absorb the scene, but I have too many questions.

"Jayce, honey," Mom says finally, trying to motion for me to come closer.

Ellie's practically sitting in her grandma's lap now, and I just feel disgusted.

"Come sit with me," Mom encourages me again. She pats the space next to her on the bed.

I stand still, staring only at the woman on the bed. Her constant smile starts to falter when she sees how I'm looking at her.

"Why are you here?" I ask point blank. My voice is clipped and hard.

"Jayce," Mom starts, but I cut her off.

"You don't belong here," I say quickly. "You should leave."

Mom's voice gathers steam. "Jayce, that's enough."

"What? Why is she here? We don't need her."

"Yes, we do," Mom says.

"We've gotten through life just fine without you," I continue. "We've never needed you all these years. Why do you think we need you now?" I know I'm being rude, and I see the hurt flash in this woman's eyes, but I can't help myself. Why are people allowed to turn their backs on us and then re-enter our lives so easily? And why am I not allowed to be mad about it? I don't have to like this woman. I don't even know her.

"Jayce! Enough."

"She cast you away, Mom. And why? Because you were having me. She didn't want us, Mom. At least, she sure didn't want me."

"I made a huge mistake," the woman says. "One that I've regretted and had to pay for dearly, for many, many years." Her voice quivers, and she struggles to keep her composure.

"Yeah, sure. That's why you tried so hard to find us and make things right." The sarcasm is undeniable, and anger surges through me uncontrollably.

"Calm down, J.J.," Mom says soothingly.

"No. I won't. And she doesn't deserve you or your love." I'm starting to shake. "What? She's going to step in and make everything better? We don't need her. We've been taking care of ourselves long enough. I've got this, Mom. Go home, lady." I give her a stony glare.

I can see that Mom's not happy with me, and the way this woman has planted herself on Mom's bed shows that she has no intention of going anywhere. I shake my head in disgust and decide it's me that'll go then, and I walk right out of the room.

Just before they are out of earshot, I hear Mom say, "It's okay. She'll come around."

No way. Not this time. I'm done letting people walk in and out of my life at their whim. It's better just to keep them out altogether.

Chapter 13

I'm sitting in a visitor lounge on the fifth floor of the hospital. The room is filled with the dim, soft light of table lamps, which is a real departure from the fluorescent lights all over the rest of the hospital. Books line shelves. Soft music plays from a stereo on one side of the room, competing with the sounds from a TV on the other side of the room. The room is meant to be calming and soothing, but I'm seething with anger and confusion. I watch an elderly man sitting in a recliner fumble with the pages of the book he's holding. His arms are shaking so badly it's a wonder he can even hold up the book, let alone turn the pages. He coughs periodically, and the cough sounds wet and rattly, similar to my mom's. I wonder if he's dying of the same thing my mom is. I stare at him longer than is polite, but right now I could care less about how I come across.

I'm shocked when an hour later I see my mom's frail figure shuffling slowly down the hallway toward the entrance to this room. She's dragging along her oxygen tank and an IV pole, and she's moving as though she's ninety-five rather than thirty-four. If it wasn't for her smooth, creamy skin and her long blond hair, she'd easily be pegged as an elderly woman in a care home.

Her face is lined with worry, and I watch her comb the halls for any sight of me. Immediately I feel guilty that I made her come and look for me.

"Jayce!" she calls out when she sees me. I stand and start to make my way toward her, when she makes it to the entrance of the lounge. She's wheezing heavily now and looks as though she might pass out.

"Mom," I admonish her. "You shouldn't be walking around like this. You can't even breathe. And you'll wear yourself out."

I take her by the arm to guide her back to her room, but she shakes me off and points to the couch in the lounge.

"Sit," she says.

I sit dutifully and watch her try to settle herself into the seat beside me. She is so weak, it's a marvel she's made it all the way to me.

"I'm sorry, Mom," I say quickly. While I'm not happy about the situation, I know that the last thing I want to do is cause my mom any more pain than what she's already experiencing.

"No. Listen," she replies. She has another long coughing fit that rivals even the man who is still fumbling with his book, but he seems oblivious to the two of us. "I called my mom. I had to. I know that I'm very sick. We DO need the help. I can't keep leaving you to take care of Ellie and our home and everything else on your own. You are sixteen years old, Jayce. It's not fair to you."

"It's not fair that she can just come back into your life as though nothing happened," I reply.

"You're right. It's not fair. A lot of things aren't fair right now. Your mom being sick. Having to take care of your little sister and still deal with school. Your dad living a life we didn't expect …" Her voice catches.

"I can do it, Mom. I've been helping do this for so long." It's true. Mom's been working double shifts for most of our lives. I've been stepping up to help ever since Joelle was born. I'm practically another mother to her, anyhow.

"It's too much, J.J. And I won't put you through any more than necessary."

"How did she get here?" I wonder.

"She drove up as soon as I called her this morning." And then she says, quieter, "Same phone number."

We both grow silent, contemplating this fact.

"She started crying as soon as she heard my voice. Told me she'd waited for this day for years."

"I don't get it. All these years she could've tried phoning you or finding you. But she didn't."

"She said she thought I'd never forgive her for what they'd done."

"Yeah, but she didn't even try. And you shouldn't forgive her. What they did was terrible."

"Jayce, it's important to give her a chance to make it right. I could only give you so much. You have so little family as it is. You can never have too many people around you loving you."

"She doesn't love me. She doesn't even know me."

"Not yet. But she will. And she'll fall in love with you just like everyone else." Mom smiles. "You're irresistible."

"No, that's Ellie," I say. Ellie always steals the show with her pageant-worthy looks and her sweet demeanour.

"I need to know that there'll be other people in your life," Mom says.

"Why? We have you. It's always been enough." I think back to the past week and how lonely I've felt. How much I've needed my mom.

"No, it's not enough, J.J. And I might not always be around," Mom whispers.

"So, it's true then? You're being moved to this new room to die? Just like that? I thought you were going to fight this thing." My voice grows higher and I find myself bristling with anger again.

"I'm trying, J.J." Mom breaks down in tears. "But I'm just so tired ..."

With that we cling to each other and I try to take in every part of her. The feeling of the small of her back as I wrap my arms around her, the floral smell of her deodorant through her plain hospital gown, her rapid heartbeat thumping steadily against my chest, the intensity of our emotions practically surging through our two bodies. She feels like a shell of her healthy self.

"Promise me you'll try," Mom whispers in my ear.

Holding her like a broken little bird in my arms, I know I'd do anything my mom asks. Anything at all. I don't have a choice.

"Okay," I whisper back.

Chapter 14

After Mom and I return to the hospital room, I try to be polite and engage in small talk. Thankfully, Ellie does most of the talking, delighting us with her antics and filling the awkward silences for us. When Mom falls asleep, our grandma says she should call for a hotel room. Although I don't want her to stay with us, I promised Mom I'd try to give this woman a chance and so it feels only right to offer our home to her instead of a hotel. Mom would want that.

When we get down to the parking lot, I buckle Ellie into the back seat of our grandma's newer red four-door sedan. I try to tighten the seat belt as much as possible because there isn't a booster seat, but the seat belt still hangs loose on her little frame. This time, our grandma does all of the talking. She seems nervous as she drives, and she's eager to fill the silence.

I learn that she's sixty-four years old and that she's a widow now. Her husband, Ernie, my grandpa, died just one year ago of a stroke at the age of sixty-eight.

"It's been so lonely without him," my grandma says.

If she is waiting for me to soothe her or ask questions about him, I don't.

"Your mom is very proud of you," my grandma offers. "She was just beaming as she described you to me." She looks over at me. I smirk. My grandma's first glimpse of me has been of someone who is seething and full of attitude.

"Guess I'm not the sweet granddaughter you expected, am I?" I say.

"You have every right to be upset and confused," my grandma replies. "This isn't how I wanted to see my daughter again and meet my grandchildren."

"You didn't even call her when her dad died," I state, incredulous.

"I should have. I know. It's just … so many years went by. I didn't know if I had a right to be in her life again."

"And yet she called you."

"Yes. And I thank God she did. I prayed for this moment for years."

"She's a better person than you," I state matter-of-factly. And she doesn't disagree.

The car is silent again except for the radio announcer's voice reading out the news stories of the day. I point to each street she needs to take to get to our house, and not another word is said.

We pull up to our modest little house. I unfasten Ellie's seat belt and help her out of the back seat. Grandma is studying our yard. The lawn is overgrown and weeds jut out in several places. Our grandma takes out a duffle bag from the trunk and follows us up the walk.

I unlock the front door and feel suddenly self-conscious at letting this woman into our home. Suddenly it feels unkempt and tired, despite my best efforts. I see how badly it needs to be swept and vacuumed and how stale the air smells. I watch our grandma's eyes scan the house, but she doesn't seem to be doing it in a disapproving way. It's like she's taking it all in and figuring out what can be done.

"It's a little messy," I say, but she doesn't seem fazed. Instead, she walks over to the bookcase in the corner and studies the three small framed photos on the shelf. She picks each one up and then gingerly sets it down. Ellie and I stand at the doorway, a bit bewildered and unsure of what to do with this stranger in our house who is examining our things.

She turns back toward us, with tears streaming down her face. "I am so, so sorry," she cries. She buries her head in her hands and her cries turn to wails of anguish. "I've lost so many years with her," she chokes. "And so many years with you."

"It's okay. You are here now," I say with far more generosity than I feel.

Ellie walks over to her and rubs her back affectionately.

"It's okay, Grandma," Ellie tells her. And this woman breaks down completely at the empathy Ellie shows her. I marvel at Ellie's ability to accept this new person so easily.

"I'd always wanted granddaughters," our grandma says through her tears.

"No, you didn't," I shoot back. "You didn't want me."

"That's not true. It's just … Eleanor was so young. She was ruining her future, getting pregnant. And that man was too old for her, and he was nothing but trouble."

Well, that's at least something we can agree on. Our dad really was nothing but trouble.

"And Ernie, my husband … your grandpa … well, he just couldn't handle it."

"So you let him make the decision, and that was that?"

"I hoped things would change. That we just needed time."

"It's been almost seventeen years. I'd say that makes your little experiment an epic fail."

I know Mom said that her dad was the ruler of the household, and was very strict, but still. I'm not about to let her off the hook that easy.

"For what it's worth, I'm here now, and I want to be a part of your lives, if you'll let me," she says hopefully.

"I don't really have a choice. But it's what Mom wants."

I spin on my heels and head to my room. I've got homework and a million other things I'm behind on. Ellie has cozied up to our grandma pretty fast. For once I can worry about myself while someone else tends to her.

I hear water running, the clanking of dishes, and other sounds while I sit in my room. I try to concentrate on my studies, but it's hard to focus. My mind is going a mile a minute, trying to process everything that's happened in the last couple of days: my best friend has dropped me, my mom's health is deteriorating rapidly, I saw my dad again after several years (and that was a disaster), and now my estranged grandma is staying in our house. This last one shocks me the most. I want to hate her and tell her to get out of here, but the more I think about having her here, the more I know we actually do need her. Or at least someone … and since there aren't any others stepping up to help out, I guess this is the best option we've got.

I lie on my bed and feel the rush of loneliness wash over me. I curl into my blankets, and tears slide slowly down my cheeks, leaving wet circles on my pillow.

Chapter 15

I wake up to sunlight streaming through my window, practically blinding me. I must have forgotten to close the blinds last night. I sit up and wipe away the drool that's collected on my chin. I'm still in the same clothes I wore yesterday.

The amazing aroma of bacon hits me, and I realize that it's being cooked in this house, right now. I can't remember the last time we had bacon. Although usually my stomach isn't much interested in food early in the day, today it's growling at the tantalizing scent.

As I open my bedroom door, I hear my grandma and Ellie chatting away. Sure enough, my grandma is wearing an apron and standing over the stove with a flipper in her hand. The bacon sizzles loudly. I can see the grease spattering up toward her hands, but she seems so enthralled with whatever Ellie is saying that she doesn't seem to notice.

"Good morning," she greets me warmly when she sees me approach.

"J.J., look!" Ellie shrieks. "Grandma's making bacon!" She's very excited about this. I can't tell if it's more about having a grandma here or having the bacon, but I suspect it's our grandma she's more excited about.

I eye my grandma warily. She takes in my appearance and my dishevelled clothes from the day before, and she smiles.

"Did you have a good sleep?"

"Uh, I guess," I answer.

"I slipped out early this morning to get some groceries. I wanted to make sure you girls had a good breakfast to start the day."

I open the fridge, and, sure enough, it's brimming with food. Far more food than we've had in months. My stomach jumps again at the sight. I think of how I've tried to convince Joelle to eat oatmeal every morning, and now there's even a box of Corn Pops sitting on the counter.

Aside from the frying pans on the stove, the kitchen is spotless. In fact, the whole house looks clean and put together. She must've been up half the night cleaning and organizing to get our house looking the way it does. She sees me scanning the house.

"I cleaned up a bit," our grandma says.

"Yeah," I mutter. Although I'm relieved and pleasantly surprised by the scene, I'm also uncomfortable with her taking over.

"I hope you don't mind," she says again.

"Whatever."

"Okay, Joelle … here is your breakfast." She sets the plate before her and the steam billows up from the plate. Joelle and I stare, practically drooling at the sight. Alongside the bacon, there is warm, buttery toast and two perfectly cooked eggs seasoned with salt and pepper. She has even added generous wedges of cantaloupe to the plate.

"And yours, dear," she says, setting a plate before me.

"Thanks," I manage. Although I rarely have an appetite in the mornings, I dig in wholeheartedly.

"What should we do today, Joelle?" she asks.

"We should go to the libarry!" Joelle answers.

"The library? Sure! We could do that. Is there anything you'd like us to pick up for you today, Jayce?"

"No, I'm good." I'm practically shovelling this food in.

She rubs her hands together and watches us eat with a look of satisfaction. I don't want to give her that pleasure, so I chew what's in my mouth and push the plate away. I stand up from my seat.

"Oh, here, I've packed a lunch for you, too." She opens the fridge and pulls out a paper bag that is neatly folded at the top.

"I don't eat lunch at school," I say. It's a big lie, since I rarely have money to go out, but she doesn't need to know that.

"Oh, you come home, then? I will have something ready for you. Just let me know what time to expect you."

"I don't come home either. Don't worry about it."

I turn to walk to my room but she shoves the bag at me another time.

"Please, take it. You never know when you might get hungry."

I want to throw the bag and tell her that I don't want her stupid lunch, but I take it anyhow and storm off to get ready for school. She's right. You never know when you might get hungry.

I'm in class long before the first bell. I sit at my desk and doodle in my notebook. When Mr. Letts walks into the room, he glances up in surprise.

"Good morning, Miss Loewen. So glad you could make it on time."

"Good morning," I reply.

Mr. Letts gives us time to write a journal entry today. I watch as others scribble their words around me. Mr. Letts is pretending to read a piece of paper he's holding as he sits at his desk, but he keeps glancing at his students — and at me in particular.

I don't want to write anything that arouses suspicion about my home life and what's going on with my mom. But then I realize that, now that my grandma is with us, there's no need to worry about that.

> My grandma came to visit us last night.
> She is a great cook. She made us a big
> breakfast this morning. I don't usually
> eat much in the morning, but it was so
> good I practically devoured it.

There. This entry is harmless. He'll never know that she's come to take care of us because my mom is battling cancer or that we'd never actually met her before yesterday. It's not three-quarters of a page, either, but it'll have to do. I slap the journal closed and sit triumphantly. The bell rings, and, when I get up from my seat, I accidentally cut Amanda off.

"Watch it!" she squeals at me in disgust. I let her pass by, and then rush out to find Kurt. He won't believe what's happened.

I walk to his homeroom class hoping to catch him, but the class is empty. I check his locker and then scan the grounds where we like to meet and sit together. I check the cafeteria, the gym, and, finally, detention, before giving up. Maybe Kurt hasn't come to school today. It feels weird without him, since we've been inseparable at school these last couple of weeks. Instead I see Amanda standing on her toes to give Luke a kiss. He smiles and pulls her closer to kiss again. I guess they are back together after all.

I slink over to the tree Kurt and I have been sitting under, and open my lunch bag. There is a sandwich, a fresh bakery bun with a bunch of fixings, wrapped tightly in plastic. There is a bag of grapes, a container of cheese and crackers, and a chocolate brownie. My stomach leaps again at the sight. I unwrap the sandwich and take a bite. It's delicious. I take one bite after another, barely chewing in between. The food is comforting and filling, and right now I need all the comfort I can get.

I look around and see groups of students scattered all over the school grounds. Not one student is sitting alone. Waves of loneliness wash over me.

"Hey, Squirt," says a familiar voice from behind me.

"Kurt!" I say, a bit too excited. "You're here!"

"Sure am. Why? Did you miss me?" he says winking.

"Not really," I shoot back, but I'm lying through my teeth. "Where were you?"

"My grandma had a doctor's appointment this morning. I just got her back home."

"Is everything okay?"

"Yeah. She seems to be forgetting a lot of things lately. The doctor asked her a few simple questions to see if she knew the answers. Some of them she couldn't answer. The doctor didn't say anything, but I know that can't be good. They're going to run some tests."

"I hope she's okay," I say.

"What about your mom?"

"Ha. Well, my mom is getting weaker every day. They've moved her into the Palliative Care Unit now. Yesterday she could barely walk or talk without gasping for air. I'm scared she's giving up."

"If your mom is anything like you, she'll be a fighter," Kurt tells me.

"She called my grandma."

"Already?" Kurt raises his eyebrows.

"We got to the hospital and she was *there*. Like, sitting on my mom's bed!"

"No way."

"Yeah, and she was trying to be all nice to us. And Mom just let her back into our lives like it was nothing."

"Did you talk with her? What is she like?"

"I mean, I tried to avoid her. I wanted her to leave, but Mom insisted she stay at our place. I had to go home with this freakin' woman. She was nice enough and all, but how do I know it isn't an act? Especially since she cast us aside once before. What? One wrong move and we're done?"

"Whoa," is all Kurt offers.

"I woke up today to a full breakfast and a spotless house. She'd even packed my lunch. I think it's all just moving a little fast for me."

"That's crazy," Kurt agrees. "But maybe she's just trying to make up for lost time."

"Lost time that was her fault. Period."

When I get home from school, my grandma has cookies and milk waiting for me like I'm the same age as Ellie. It seems ridiculous, but I thank her and eat the cookies anyhow, because they look so good. Joelle seems really happy, and she tells me all about her day with Grandma, which included the library, ice cream, a shopping trip, and a visit to the park.

It sounds like our grandma is a better babysitter than Mrs. Johnson, and it's good for Ellie to have someone to play with all day. If there is anything good I can admit about this situation, this would be it.

Supper is already simmering on the stove. It looks like some kind of hearty stew with big chunks of meat and vegetables.

"Did your mom cook dinner for you guys?" our grandma asks.

"How else would we eat?" I retort.

She doesn't miss a beat. "I mean, did you sit down to have supper together every night?"

The truth was we didn't have supper together very often. Mom worked double shifts most nights, and she had to race from one job to the other. Most of the time, she'd eat at the diner, because Lou and Freida let their employees eat for free. I'd often heat up a can of something on the stove or pop in a microwave dinner. But I know my mom knows how to cook. I'm sure she'd make us amazing meals if she had the time.

"Mom works two jobs in order to make ends meet," I point out. "She can't sit at home and play the little homemaker."

"Maybe we should bring some of this to your mom," our grandma says, ignoring my cutting comment. "This stew was always one of her favourites."

"Yeah, well a lot has changed in seventeen years," I remind her.

Our grandma stirs the stew. She seems oblivious to my remarks.

When we eat, the stew is flavourful and delicious, but I don't tell her so. She scoops a portion of it into a container to bring to the hospital. Except for Ellie humming to herself, we remain silent during the drive to the hospital. After we park, Joelle skips alongside our grandma, the two of them holding hands. I walk several steps behind them, feeling like an outsider.

When we get up to Mom's room, our grandma gives her a hug before we can. She sets the container of stew down in front of her, and Mom lights up.

"Oh, I love this stuff," she gushes. I notice that her hospital meal is sitting untouched. She pops the lid off the stew and eagerly scoops a spoonful into her mouth. "Mmm ..." she moans. She takes two more scoops and then sets her spoon down on her hospital tray. She leans back into her pillow and closes her eyes. Three bites of stew is hardly a meal. I want to spoon it for her until her plate is clean. Maybe she'd put on some weight and be stronger. Maybe it would help her fight this. Instead, Mom wants to drift off to sleep.

We stand around her and watch as she settles into a soft snore. I can't believe that we've only just arrived and she's going to sleep. Now we can't talk and get caught up. I miss her. I want to tell her about Kurt, and what's happening with Amanda. I want her to sit up and smile and sing and hold us and tell us everything will be all right. I even want her to encourage me to get to know my grandma, just as long as she's awake and talking to me.

An hour passes. Ellie is getting restless in this tiny hospital room.

"Girls ... maybe we should go," our grandma says. Mom seems to be resting comfortably, and although I'd like to wait for her to wake up, I'm not sure when that'll happen.

I lean over my mom and kiss her forehead.

"I love you," I whisper. Tears prick my eyelids as I say it. I wish she could feel just how much love I have for her, but she doesn't even move.

Chapter 16

On Monday morning, I receive my journal back from Mr. Letts. I flip it open to my latest entry and find his comment:

> Most grandmas tend to have a knack for cooking, don't they? My own grandma was a lousy cook who often kept food years after its expiry date. We all thought we'd get sick. We'd try to take her out for dinner whenever we saw her so we didn't have to eat at her house. You are lucky to have a grandma who can cook. It sounds like she really cares about you, since breakfast IS the most important meal of the day.

His response catches me off guard, and I smile. Little does he know that my grandma only started caring about me less than a week ago, and that I really don't know much about the woman. I picture him staring at his grandma's mouldy meals and I feel a little better knowing that mine can cook. I look up from my journal, and Mr. Letts and I exchange smiles.

Kurt doesn't show up for school again. I try calling him at home, but no one answers.

It is Thursday before I see Kurt again. There are dark circles under his eyes, and he isn't as talkative as usual.

"Kurt!" I run toward him and he opens his arms for a hug. He gives me a wry smile, but he seems subdued. "Where have you been?"

"It's my grandma," he replies. "She's getting worse."

I nod and lace my fingers through his. I want to hear more.

"She fell on Sunday. She broke her hip, and she's black and blue practically everywhere."

"Oh no!" I gasp.

"I had taken a nap, and she thought she could try and go for a walk, but of course she needed help. Her fall woke me up. I went running to her. She kept saying she was going to visit her daughter and her husband because they'd just had a baby."

I look at him quizzically.

"Jayce, she meant me. I'm the baby she's talking about! She thought it was 1997."

"Oh, Kurt, I'm so sorry." Kurt's brow is furrowed and his eyes are downcast. I can feel his hand shaking a bit in mine.

"It's worse than I thought," he admits. "She's going to be in the hospital for a while."

"How come you didn't call me? I could've come to help," I say.

A small smile escapes his lips. "Yeah, okay, J.J. 'Cause you're not going through things yourself, right?"

"I'll always be here for you, no matter what."

We grow silent and walk down the hallway together. I wish Kurt was his happy, joking self. We turn toward the stairs that lead to the school's front entrance. The stairwell is empty so I bound down the stairs two at a time. When I get to the bottom, I realize that Kurt hasn't followed. I turn back. He is sitting on the top step with his head in his hands.

"Kurt?" I call back to him. I race back up to the top and put my arm around him. He reaches for my hand. "Kurt?" I repeat. I feel his body shudder and his hand grips mine tighter. He is crying. I don't know what to say. He looks up at me, with pain on his tear-stained face.

"What if she forgets me for good?"

Chapter 17

The next week passes uneventfully. I go to school, head to the hospital after supper with Joelle and our grandma, and then come home and try to focus on my homework. Mom's health is not improving, and she spends more time sleeping with each passing day. She lights up every time she sees us, and I know she wishes she could be at home with us, too.

Kurt has also been spending as much time as he can at the hospital with his grandma. With both of our loved ones in different hospitals, we talk as often as we can. It feels like we're a lifeline for each other these days — we help each other try to make sense of what's going on as the people we love the most are slipping away from us.

Our grandma is still cleaning, making meals, and taking care of us. Although she keeps trying to connect with me, I hold her at a distance. She and Ellie have grown quite close, and Ellie rarely wants to be with me anymore, now that our grandma is around. It makes me a little sad, but I know it's good for Ellie. As much as I don't want to admit it, having someone here to take care of things has made life a lot easier.

In just a couple of weeks, school will be out for the summer, and I'll be able to spend more time with my mom.

Or, at least, that's what I think will happen.

One night, our grandma sits Ellie and I down to talk.

"Well, girls, as you know, I drove here rather quickly when your mom called and asked for me to come."

I glare at her. "So?"

"Well, I've been away from Meadow Lake for quite a while now, and it's time I go back. I have to take care of some things at home and pick up some things to bring back here with me."

"So go," I mutter. Already she's had enough of us and is looking for a way out. "We're fine here without you."

Ellie starts to cry. "No, Grandma! Don't go! I want you to stay!" She jumps onto her lap and wraps her tiny arms around our grandma's neck.

"You're going to come with me," she replies.

"What?!" I shriek.

"You girls are going to come back to Meadow Lake with me."

"No. No way. There is NO way I'm going to Meadow Lake with you. What about school? What about Mom? Who will take care of her?"

"I've already discussed it with your mother. She doesn't want you here alone."

"I'm staying here. I have school!"

"We'll just be gone for a couple of days, and then we'll come back here."

Ellie claps her hands and kisses our grandma on the cheek.

"Jayce, you don't have a choice. You'll have to pack your bag tonight, because we are leaving right after school tomorrow."

I stand from the couch and stomp to my room and slam my bedroom door behind me with as much force as I can. It makes a loud bang that scares Ellie, and I hear our grandma consoling her afterward.

I can't go to Meadow Lake. I don't want to go to her home. What if she doesn't bring us back? What if her plan is to keep us there? What if she wants to punish my mom for all those years of estrangement by taking us away from her? What if something happens to Mom while we're gone? How will I talk to Kurt?

I think of walking out of the house. I could run away. I could hide out somewhere, and she'd have no choice but to head to Meadow Lake without me. *She'd probably call the police*, I realize. *I wouldn't get far.* I try to brainstorm ways to get out of going, but, in the end, I realize that I probably don't have a choice. I'll have to go. It'll only be for a couple of days. I'll go to protect Ellie.

The next afternoon we make the three-hour drive to Meadow Lake. I stare at the landscape as we drive. I like the bright yellow patches of prairie that stand out among the grain fields and the dark-green grass. We can see the sky and the land for miles and miles as we drive. It looks so open and picturesque.

As we get closer to Meadow Lake, our landscape changes drastically. We become surrounded by dense forest. The trees are thick and majestic, and we even see deer and a moose cross the road at different points in time. It almost feels like I'm about to enter another world, only because our grandma's house is as foreign to us as this forested landscape. I'm getting more nervous the closer we get.

Then suddenly the forest ends and the landscape breaks wide open again. We drive for a little while longer, and then I see the sign welcoming visitors to Meadow Lake. Our grandma turns down the first street she comes upon and heads through town without stopping. We end up on a dirt road that is heavily treed, and I start to wonder where she's actually taking us.

"We're here," she says, pulling into a yard just off the road. Trees surround the entire property.

"This is like in the middle of nowhere," I point out.

"It's very peaceful here," she says. "You might like it."

I look up at the two-storey house. It has light-yellow siding with white trim, and there are baskets of flowers hanging everywhere. On the wraparound porch, there are rocking chairs adorned with blankets and throw pillows. Everything is well-kept and tidy. It looks like a pretty nice place.

"This is where your mother grew up," our grandma tells us, opening Ellie's car door. Ellie jumps out of the car and runs toward the house.

"I want to see Mommy's room."

"I can show you her room," our grandma says. "Just let me get our things out of the car."

I grab a couple of our bags and follow our grandma into her house. I can't believe I am standing in our grandparents' home, in the house where my mom spent her childhood. How would Mom feel coming back to this place? Would this bring her comfort or pain?

The inside of the house looks like a rustic cottage, with its pine siding, hardwood floors, and wooden kitchen cabinets. There are a lot of windows, so it feels bright and airy. It is immaculately clean. Some photos line the walls, but mostly I see wooden crosses and plaques of Jesus and Mary. I step closer to the photos, hoping to catch a glimpse of my mom and her brother in their youth, but the photos are of older people.

"Those are your great-grandparents." She catches me studying the photos. I don't see any resemblance to us.

"This is your mom. And your uncle." She picks up a photo frame beside the couch. It is the same photo that Mom has in the box hidden in her closet.

"You know, I didn't even know she had a brother until about two weeks ago."

"Really? She never talked about him?"

"No. I found a box of her keepsakes, and this picture was in it. I asked her about it, and then she told me what happened to him."

"It was really hard on Eleanor." Our grandma swallows and takes a deep breath. "It was hard on all of us."

Her body shakes with emotion and she blinks back the tears that begin to erupt.

"Then you shut her out, too. She had no one. No wonder she ran off with my dad."

"She thought your dad was the best thing to happen to her. We had our doubts about him. And she was so young.... How long did your dad stick around?"

"Longer than you did."

"Jayce, I swear to you, I'll spend the rest of my life making that mistake up to you and your sister. And your mom."

"Where's her room?"

"It's upstairs. Follow me." Ellie and I trail behind her up the stairs. She stops at the door closest to the staircase and swings it open.

Ellie and I step gingerly into the room. The walls are a soft peach colour, and posters of teenage stars are taped onto the wall beside her bed. I don't recognize any of them. There is a corkboard over a desk that has pictures of Mom and her friends tacked onto it. Jewellery is stacked in piles on her desk. There are stuffed animals on her bed, which is neatly made and ready to sleep in. Even her slippers are lined up by the door. What catches me the most are the dozens of drawings that adorn the rest of the space. Ellie and I don't say a word. We just take it all in.

"It's not much different," our grandma says. "I kept everything the same over the years, in case she ever came back home." She walks over to one of Mom's drawings and pulls it gently from the wall.

"Your mom is very talented. She always loved to draw."

We stare at the sketch of a young girl, most likely in her early teens, standing at a window and looking out at a stormy sky. "I see you love to draw, too," our grandma says. How does she know this about me?

I picture my mom sitting at that desk, working hard on her art. I picture her lying on her bed, daydreaming like teenage girls do. I picture her learning she's pregnant and feeling scared, knowing that her parents might not let her stay. I picture her glancing around this room for the last time, and wonder if she had sensed she'd never be back.

"If you would like to stay in this room tonight, you're welcome to," she says to me.

I smile and drop the bag I'm holding. Yup, this room is mine.

Chapter 18

Ellie and I explore the huge lot the next day while our grandma does laundry and makes phone calls. Later in the day, she brings us frosty glasses of iced tea that feel slippery in our warm hands. We play hide-and-seek in the dense shrubs and trees that surround the property while our grandma waters her garden and pulls weeds. She looks at us from time to time and smiles.

In the corner of the yard, a swing is tethered to wooden beams almost as high as the second storey of the house. We take turns pushing each other. It feels great to act like a kid again.

"Your grandpa built that when we bought this house," our grandma says. Even though my mom said her parents were super strict, I can't help but feel like this house would've been a great place to grow up.

That night, I snuggle into my mom's bed. It feels weird but also comforting. Mom knew I was coming here. They'd already arranged it. Did Mom want us to see this place? Did she want us to better understand where she'd come from?

When hours go by without sleep, I decide to call Kurt. It is about one in the morning, and the house has been quiet for a long time. I tiptoe down the hallway, trying to be careful not to wake anyone, but the floor creaks beneath my feet and threatens to give me away. I head down to the kitchen, to my grandma's cordless phone that is mounted next to the refrigerator. Kurt picks up on the first ring.

"Kurt, it's me, Jayce," I whisper.

"Jayce? Where are you? I've been trying to call you!"

"I'm at my grandma's in Meadow Lake. I had no choice, but it's only until Monday."

"I'm so glad you called." His voice is wavering. Something is wrong.

"Kurt, what is it?"

"She's gone, Jayce," he sobs. "My grandma passed away this morning."

"Oh, Kurt." My voice shakes with emotion. "I'm so sorry."

"What am I going to do without her? I don't have anyone." His cries stab at my heart.

"You've got me," I offer, but then instantly regret the words. How could I even think I could be a substitute for the woman who has cared for him his whole life?

"The funeral is going to be on Wednesday. It's at 10:30 a.m. at St. Mary's."

I listen as Kurt talks about his grandma, about how wonderful she was to him. I want to be there to hug him and listen to him in person. How could I be stuck in Meadow Lake instead?

"I'll be there, Kurt. I promise."

I say goodbye and slink back to my mom's room to try and get some sleep.

"We need to go back to Saskatoon," I inform Ellie and our grandma at the breakfast table the next morning. I'm breathless and stammering. "It's really important. My friend's grandma died, and she was practically a mother to him. She was all he had, and he was the one taking care of her, and now she died, and I need to go back …" I'm practically shouting and then I lose all control. I hold my head in my hands and let the tears come.

"Okay," our grandma says simply. "Let's pack up."

Chapter 19

On the day of the funeral, I skip school. My grandma drives me to the church.

"Are you sure you don't want me to come with you?" she asks for about the tenth time.

"No, it's okay."

I sit in a pew close to the doors. I watch as people shuffle in. A hymn is being played on the organ, but nobody is singing along. A few people dab at their eyes with tissues. There is a large photo of Kurt's grandma on display near the altar, surrounded by dozens of colourful flower arrangements.

I study the funeral card. It reads: "Ada Friesen (1944–2015)." The card has several pictures of her with Kurt at various points of his childhood. They look so happy and close. Although I never got the chance to meet her, I feel some sort of kinship with her. Perhaps it's our mutual love for Kurt. My stomach flops at the thought of seeing him.

The priest asks everyone to stand, and the organist starts a new song.

Kurt steps through the doors alone; he's holding a small box of what must be his grandma's ashes. His face is drawn and sombre. His jaw is set. He makes his way to the front of the church and sets the box down beside his grandma's photo.

One of Ada's friends from church gives the eulogy and describes her as a vibrant woman, full of life. She'd been a florist during her working years and believed that flowers could brighten anyone's day. *She would've loved all the flowers here,* I think to myself. I learn that although she'd been married at a young age, she'd lost her husband in an industrial accident. She became a single parent to a five-year-old and never remarried. Her greatest joy in life was her grandson, Kurt, whom she raised from the age of two. And, the eulogist continues, Kurt turned out to be her biggest blessing, as well, as he took care of Ada when her health started to fail, even though he was just a teenager himself.

Kurt is sitting in the first row with his head down. I can see his shoulders shaking at times. Finally, I can't take it anymore, being so far away from him and watching him in so much pain. I get up from my seat and walk up to the front pew. I slide in beside Kurt and wrap my arm around him. He settles into my shoulder.

"Thank you, J.J.," he manages.

At the end of the service, I watch as Kurt shakes hands with people and makes small talk. He looks so handsome and distinguished. I wonder if his grandma is smiling at his polished appearance, so different from his usual leather jacket, unkempt hair, and Converse shoes. That is the true Kurt, though — the one I love best.

I can tell Kurt doesn't want to be there anymore, but greeting everyone and thanking them for attending is the polite thing to do. I want to wait for everyone to leave, but people keep milling around. Kurt makes a dash toward me when he gets the chance.

"Thanks for coming, Jayce."

"I wouldn't be anywhere else, Kurt." We stand hugging.

"I don't know when I'm going to get out of here. You should just go home," he says.

"Are you sure? I don't mind waiting."

"No, just go home. I'm okay. I'll call you later." I nod and we say goodbye.

As I walk down the steps of the church, a car honks. It is my grandma, waving me over.

"How did you … have you been waiting here the whole time?" I ask.

"I came right back after I dropped you off. I wanted to make sure you got home okay. I didn't want you to be alone."

"Where's Ellie?"

"She's with Mrs. Johnson. Turns out Mrs. Johnson's been missing having her around and was happy to watch her."

I slide into the passenger seat, and we both watch Kurt in front of the church.

"I'm sorry he has to go through so much," my grandma says. During the car ride back to Saskatoon, I had ended up telling her all about Kurt. She knows that he has been taking care of his grandma for a long time, and that he has lost the closest thing to a mother he has ever known. The car pulls out of the parking spot, and I wave to Kurt as we pass him.

"Why don't you invite him over for supper tonight?"

"Sure!" I say quickly. My grandma stops the car and I run out toward Kurt.

"Wanna come for supper when you're all done here? No pressure. I understand if you're not up to it." But Kurt looks relieved and touched that I'd ask. I get the sense he doesn't want to be alone.

"I'll come over as soon as I can." Kurt and I hug again, and then I run back to the car.

"Is he a love interest?" My grandma's curiosity is getting the best of her.

"No. It's not like that with us," I say. "He's my best friend."

Chapter 20

When I get to school on Thursday, Amanda taps me on the shoulder just before class begins.

"Jayce, I have to talk to you."

My heart is hammering in my chest. I've had enough of Amanda's snubs and I'm not up for whatever mean game she has planned. Sensing my reluctance, she adds, "I just found out about your mom. I'm SO sorry, Jayce."

My eyes grow wide.

"I haven't been a good friend to you at all. I was so caught up in my own drama that I didn't see that you needed me, too. Kurt told me everything," she finishes.

Kurt? Why is Kurt talking to Amanda?

"Why didn't you tell me what was happening?"

I have no answer for her.

"I've been horrible to you. I'm so sorry."

I look her in the eye. She looks genuinely upset. In fact, she looks as though she might cry, and something about that feels good.

"It's okay," I say.

She stands, waiting, hoping I'll say more, but I don't.

"So, we're good then?" She's wringing her hands and biting her lip.

"Yeah, we're good." I sit down in my desk, open my notebook, and pretend she's not there.

When it's time to write in our journals, I know just what to write:

> If your so-called friends betray you, that is the worst of all. Trust isn't a given. It's earned. And until you have experienced what it's like to lose a friend, you can't really appreciate what true friendship looks like. Sure, you can have friends for all kinds of different reasons in your life. Some are great for having fun, some are better for confiding in than others, and some know you so well they become practically like family. Rarely does a friend come along who can be all of these things and more. True friendship is hard to find.

"Kurt, what are you doing talking to Amanda?" I confront him when I see him after school.

"I thought she should know what's going on." He seems unfazed by my annoyance.

"I could've told her myself if I wanted her to know."

"I knew you'd be upset over this. Jayce, you need all the support you can get right now. You might lose your mom, and, if you do, you're going to want Amanda around. You'll want anyone who supports you around when it happens. Trust me, I know."

I cross my arms and stare at him. "I could've handled it myself."

"No, Jayce, you couldn't have, because you are stubborn. And you don't let people in. How can people support you if they don't even know what's going on?"

"Oh, so this is about me? You said yourself you didn't think Amanda was a very good friend to me. What changed your mind?"

"I just know how hard it is to lose someone you love. I thought if Amanda really was a good friend, she'd see that she'd made a mistake and she'd make things right. Did she?"

"I don't need you fixing things for me, Kurt. I'm a big girl. I can handle things myself." I grab my backpack and sling it over my shoulder. I don't need this. All of these people thinking they know what's best for me. I'm done with it.

"Mom, you have to get better," I beg her. I am sitting on her bed, painting her fingernails. She smiles and takes a big breath. I'm visiting my mom on my own, and it's so nice to have her to myself.

"That looks pretty," she says, looking down at the pale pink I've brushed on. "How are things going with your grandma?"

"I'm trying, Mom." That's all I want to say.

"She really cares about you two," Mom tells me.

I nod.

"There's a lot Ellie doesn't understand," Mom continues.

I nod again.

"I know you'll make sure she's taken care of, too."

"Mom, quit talking like this." I finish with her other hand and blow on her nails gently to get them to dry. "You'll be out of here before you know it, and we'll be singing and dancing around the house, just like old times." I can tell Mom is thinking of a memory of us. She is smiling.

"You never did tell me what you thought of Meadow Lake," Mom says.

"Your mom kept your bedroom the exact same!" I tell her. "You could go back there and be seventeen all over again!" We both laugh. "I even slept in your bed. It was a pretty nice place."

"It's been so long since I've been back there." Her voice is wistful. She closes her eyes again, as though she is imagining it all in her mind.

As I finish my homework that night, the doorbell rings. I assume it is Kurt, so I throw open the door. I feel bad about how I treated him today, and I want to apologize.

But the person standing in the doorway isn't Kurt. It's my dad. He's clean-shaven and dressed in neatly pressed clothes. His eyes soften at the sight of me. He's holding his hat in his hands.

I stand frozen. Ellie is already asleep, so she will be saved from this encounter.

"Who's at the door?" my grandma calls out. She senses that something is wrong and comes up behind me.

"Joe Loewen." My grandma is almost as speechless as I am.

"Mrs. Nichols," my dad says politely.

"You decided to show your face around here?" Her voice is curt.

"I had to make sure these girls were all right."

"These girls are your daughters." *This can't be happening right now. I must be dreaming.*

"I know."

"You haven't made sure they're all right their whole lives."

I take a step back and swallow the lump in my throat. I don't want to be part of this conversation.

"You're the reason Eleanor left in the first place. Don't play the doting grandma with me. You haven't been around either."

"You took her from me!" my grandma says.

"No — you did that to yourself, by forcing her away," my dad says.

"You were trouble from the start, and we knew it."

"I admit I didn't give her the life she deserved. But I loved her."

"You didn't give her that either. Where have you been while she has been in the worst fight of her life?"

"Stop!" I break in. Ellie has come out of her room. She looks terrified. She is clutching her blanket for dear life and watching us with huge eyes.

The two of them look at me with surprise, and then see Ellie standing there. They clamp their mouths shut. I go to Ellie and scoop her up. "It's okay," I say, soothing her.

"Come in and sit down. We're not going to get anything accomplished yelling in the doorway," my grandma says. We all find ourselves a seat in the living room. I feel remarkably calm.

"Why are you here?" I ask my dad.

"I've been worried about you. I had to make sure that you were okay."

"It's a little late for worries. We've been taking care of ourselves for years. What made you think that would change just because we learned the truth about you?"

He hangs his head down.

"I love you, Jayce. You're my Jaybird …"

"I am NOT your Jaybird. That girl's been gone for years. Does Mallory know you're here?" I demand.

"Who's Mallory?" my grandma interjects.

"Yes. She wants me to be here. It wouldn't be right otherwise."

I laugh a high-pitched laugh. My dad is telling me about right and wrong and making good on something?

"Mallory is his wife," I say to my grandma. "They have a four-year-old daughter together. It turns out that my dad isn't a successful touring musician as he led us to believe all these years. He lives in P.A. with an entirely different family."

My grandma's jaw drops open. I look back at my dad.

"We're fine. We don't need you."

"Jayce, I'd like to be a part of your lives. I'd like to get to know Joelle. I want to have a relationship with you. I know I have a lot to make up to you."

I picture us moving into his home in Prince Albert, being added to his perfect family life with Mallory and Maddie. It's not that easy. Life doesn't work that way.

"Go back to your family, Joe," my grandma says quietly.

"I won't. They are my daughters, too. I have a right to them."

"You gave up that right long ago."

"How about you? Why do you get to walk back in?"

"Eleanor wants me here."

"I want to see Eleanor, too."

"Over my dead body." Despite my dad's height, my grandma's words stand over him. The air is charged with emotion. I feel like we could power the house with the atmosphere we've created. I pull on my grandma's arm to get her to sit down again. He is NOT going to see my mom. At least my grandma and I agree on that.

"I am their father. You can't keep me from them," my dad says.

"I will do whatever I have to do to make sure these girls are safe."

"Oh, bloody hell, I'm not going to hurt them, Elsa."

"You've been lying to them their whole lives. How do I know you're telling the truth now?"

Dad shakes his head in disgust.

"Why are you two doing this? And pretending we don't exist? We're right here," I remind them.

"She's right," my grandma says. The room is quiet. We sit in silence for several minutes.

"I'd like the girls to stay with me." My grandma looks over at me, and then adds, "If they want to."

It hits me that staying in our own home doesn't sound like it's a choice. Is this what it's going to come down to? Moving to Prince Albert or to Meadow Lake to live with my dad or my grandma? Why are they talking like this?

"What about Mom?"

Both my grandma's and my dad's eyes fill with tears as they look at me.

I believed that she was fighting this, that there was a chance she'd get better. Why are they so sure she's going to die? Their faces look so sad, I wonder if they've ever believed she had a chance to survive.

I get it. We're planning for life without Mom. Somehow everyone got the memo but me.

Chapter 21

When I get to school on Monday morning, the strangest thing happens. Random people are approaching me and patting me on the back or giving me a hug. "We're sorry to hear about your mom being sick," they tell me. I grip my binder tighter to me and thank each person for their well wishes. How does everyone know about my mom? Is this Kurt again?

In my homeroom class, Mr. Letts pats me on my shoulder and says he's sorry that my mom is ill. "Maybe I was too hard on you this term, Miss Loewen ... given everything that's been going on."

I am incredulous. But I tell him it is fine, that I should still be in class on time. I make my way to my desk and my journal is waiting for me. When I open my journal, I see his remarks:

True courage is looking in the face of adversity and deciding that you'll stand firm. Sometimes things are thrust upon us that we may not be ready for and that we may not understand. Know that your formidable strength will carry you through. PS Having some of those true friends you wrote about will help as well.

The words blur from the tears that well in my eyes. I can't bring myself to look up. It feels like the whole room is staring at me and watching my every move. I don't feel like I'm a freak show or anything, though. I feel like I'm being enveloped in warmth and love.

Amanda walks into the classroom. Kurt is behind her, and he hands her a stack of papers that she starts putting on everyone's desk. I was rotten to Kurt the other day and I owe him an apology. We catch eyes and he smiles at me. His eyes tell me that he forgives me and that everything is all right. Amanda looks over at Mr. Letts, who nods at her, and then she turns to the class and clears her throat.

"As you all know, every year our school organizes a fundraiser. We've decided that this year we will put on a fundraiser for cancer, in support of Jayce Loewen's mom, who is battling this awful disease. There will be a barbecue on the last day of school. The teachers have agreed to cook all of the food. Volunteers will be collecting donations in the cafeteria over the lunch hour every day this week and all the proceeds will go to the Canadian Cancer Society. Please give generously and help spread the word."

The class erupts in applause. This is Amanda at her best, organizing for a good cause, pulling together all the right people to make something incredible happen. It's the reason I wanted to be her friend in the first place. She is generous and has a big heart, and I know she's the reason I've been receiving all of this newfound support.

I wipe the tears that are falling down my cheeks and head toward her. She starts to cry, and pulls me in for a big hug.

"I'm so sorry, Jayce. I'll do anything I can to help."

"I know," I tell her. "Thanks. Honestly, I mean it. Thank you."

Other students join us at the front and put their arms around me.

"Group hug!" Mr. Letts calls out, and we all start laughing.

I've learned something today. Support can come from where you least expect it.

Chapter 22

Kurt comes over for supper again. He's been having a hard time being all alone in his grandma's house, so he's been spending a lot of time over at our place. In fact, he's with us practically every night. My grandma doesn't mind. In fact, she adores his sense of humour and good nature. Their playful banter brings Ellie and me lots of laughter. Some nights we actually have fun. It's like he's become a member of the family. He's even been coming to the hospital with us. Even though his grandma's passing is so fresh, he says he wants to be there for me. In a way, he's made us all stronger.

At the moment, he is taking Ellie on an airplane ride on his back. They are zooming around the house and she is giggling uncontrollably. The sound is like music to all of our ears.

"Is my dad coming by tonight?" I ask my grandma.

My dad's been staying in a hotel. He's been here for over a week. I wonder what Mallory and his daughter think of this; I wonder if they are begging for him to come home to them. My grandma has been allowing him to come over for short periods of time, but she has asked that he stay away from the hospital.

"How do you feel about this?" she asks me.

"I don't really know," I admit. "He is my dad. I've waited more than half my life for him to want to be here with us. Now that he's here, I'm just not sure."

My grandma nods in understanding. "Kind of like how you must feel about me."

I manage a smile.

"I just want to do what's right for you and your sister."

"Why do you get to decide that?" I ask.

"Well, I guess I want to decide that with you. Your mother gets the ultimate decision."

"I want to hate you." The words are crisp and clear and plain as day. "You're not supposed to be here. You don't get to just walk into someone's life and expect them to welcome you with open arms, especially when you cast them away to begin with."

She listens, nodding gently.

"I want to tell you to go, that we don't need you. That I don't even want you here." My face scrunches up, and the tears cascade. "But you take good care of us and you've been kind and helpful and you're trying so hard. And I want to hate you. SO badly! And I can't."

"I know, Jayce. I know," she cries. "I don't deserve to be here. I don't. But I'm lucky enough to be here and I don't want to mess this up. I know it's hard to believe, but I love you. I do. You will always be my family whether you accept me or not. And I will spend the rest of my life regretting what I did so many years ago. Now that I've been given this chance, I see everything I've missed and it BREAKS my heart. You girls are the most amazing things to ever happen to me."

"But we were always here all along! We didn't just happen to you."

"I know. And you can hate me. Lord knows I deserve it."

"But don't you see? I want to hate you. And I can't!" I cry hysterically. "Instead I start to love you. And what if you walk away again? What if we don't measure up? What then?"

"Oh, honey, there's nothing to measure up to. You are perfect the way you are. And I'll never walk away. EVER. I promise." Her body heaves with the intensity of her sobs. "I love you, too!"

She pulls me close and we sit embracing for a long time. Her arms feel strong and reassuring around me. Solid. Sure.

When we arrive at the hospital that night, Mom is sitting up and alert. She has some colour on her cheeks. Her hair has been washed and brushed, and it gleams like spun sunlight. She looks like an angel in that stark hospital room.

"My girls!" she greets us. She puts her arms out and we run toward her. She is smiling at her mom, and she welcomes Kurt, as well, when she sees him trailing behind.

"You are looking well," my grandma remarks. She kisses her daughter on the forehead and smooths the top of her hair.

"I feel good," Mom says. "How are things at home?" Her eyes dart back and forth between my grandma and me. It's as though she can sense the change between us. The two of us smile and look back at her.

"It's good," I say. My grandma reaches for my hand and gives it a squeeze. My mom lights up.

"I'm glad," she says, and I know she means it.

Dr. Maniah comes into the room and sees us all gathered around Mom's bed.

"We've got the whole crew here," she remarks. We all smile and watch as she examines Mom gently. "You are looking stunning today, Eleanor. Ready for some dancing?" she asks.

Mom smiles. "Maybe. I think it's time I talk with my family though."

"Are you sure?" Dr. Maniah pats her hand. Mom nods. She swallows. We all look at her expectantly.

"I want to go home."

"I think the hospital is the best place for you, dear," my grandma says.

Ellie perks up. "Mommy can come home?"

"How can she come home?" I wonder.

Dr. Maniah chooses her words carefully. She looks specifically at Ellie and me. "Your mom is still really sick. Because she's been in the hospital for a really long time, she wants to go somewhere more comfortable." It sounds reasonable, but I know there's more to it.

"What about the medicine and the treatments?" My voice is tinged with panic. She's only just started receiving chemotherapy and radiation.

"Yes, Eleanor, what about the treatments?" my grandma's voice is just as on edge as mine is.

"I want to stop."

With those four simple words it is as though all the air has been sucked out of the room at once. I feel the magnitude of what this means. I want to run — down the hall, down the street, down to the other side of the world. But I know running won't help.

"I want to experience my last days with my family. I want to feel the sun on my face again, the scent of the breeze. I want to watch my girls running and playing. I want to listen to music and look at the stars. I want to take in everything I can." Mom talks with such conviction I know she's been thinking about this for a while now.

"Well, we could get the supports we need in place at the house and we can drive back and forth for treatment. We don't have to stop everything," my grandma says. She is barely holding herself together.

Dr. Maniah looks over at Mom. They have an understanding that the rest of us aren't getting.

"No, Mom. You don't understand," Mom says. "I want to go *home*. To Meadow Lake."

Chapter 23

On the last day of school, students and staff are scattered everywhere. The school grounds have been decorated with white streamers and balloons. White ribbons are being distributed, and I learn that they represent lung cancer awareness. My heart swells at the sight. Amanda sees me and comes running.

"Jayce, we're over six hundred dollars already and we haven't even had the barbecue yet!" She's practically jumping up and down. "Come, I want to show you something." She grabs me by the hand and I follow her to the main tables where the food will be laid out. Tacked up against the side of the school is a large poster. On it are signatures and messages from teachers and students.

I stand in wonder. Can this really be happening? There are probably hundreds of signatures and kind messages for me and my family.

"I know it's not much, but I thought it might bring you some comfort," Amanda says.

I nod, brushing tears from my eyes, and I hug her. "It's perfect."

By the end of the day, the fundraiser has hit a total of $1,836, which is pretty amazing for a school in a humble little neighbourhood. Amanda asks for all the students to gather around the podium they've set up outside. Mr. Letts sees me standing in the crowd and walks over to me.

"You take good care of yourself," he tells me. "I wish you much strength as you take care of your mom."

"Thanks, Mr. Letts. I will. Thanks for your support. I really appreciate it." He pats me on the back and moves through the crowd.

The student council delivers a thank-you speech and then the principal wishes everyone a good summer. The students hoot and holler with joy at this signal for the start of summer holidays, and many of them rush off the school grounds at once.

Amanda starts packing up the audio equipment and dismantling the podium while other staff and students stay to clean up from the barbecue.

"Thanks again, Amanda. This was all so amazing."

"I'm so sorry I wasn't there for you through all of this. I was so mean. I acted in a lot of ways I'm not proud of."

"You were going through your own stuff, too," I reason.

"No, not stuff like this. I was so caught up in trying to get Luke back, I forgot all about my friends."

"And now you guys are back together."

"No, we're done."

"Weren't you guys kissing in the hallway a couple of weeks ago?"

"Trust me. It's over. You were SO right about him. Let's just say it took me way too long to come to my senses." Amanda laughs. "I should've listened to you right from the beginning."

I'm glad that Amanda's moved on from him. This girl is the Amanda I know.

"What about you?" she asks me in a playful voice. "Are you and Kurt an item?"

"Nah, it's not like that with us," I say. "But he's one of the best things to ever happen to me."

"I'm happy for you," Amanda says, and the way she's looking into my eyes, I believe her.

"I guess I should tell you the news," I start. "I won't be coming back here."

"What?! What do you mean? Back where?"

"Back to this school. I'm leaving the city."

Amanda's face falls.

"I'm going to live at my grandma's in Meadow Lake. We're all going. My mom wants to stop treatment and spend her last days there."

"I wish you weren't going," she says. We stand quietly looking at each other for a moment or two. "Promise me you'll stay in touch?"

"Of course," I tell her.

"Don't forget your message board," she says. A teacher has taken it down and rolled it up for me to take home.

"I won't." I smile. Once I grab the poster board I glance back at the school, taking it all in. I wonder what my new school will be like, if I'll make friends. I wonder if I'll ever be back here, or if this is goodbye forever.

Chapter 24

The car is silent except for the hum of Mom's oxygen tank and soft snores from Ellie, who is slumped on my shoulder. A small U-Haul trailer is attached to the car, and it is packed solid with our things. Mom is sitting on the front passenger's side. Her seat is reclined slightly to help her feel more comfortable. I keep studying her from the back seat, looking for signs of distress now that we've taken her from the hospital. I can tell my grandma is nervous about bringing my mom back here, too. We pull up to the yellow two-storey house, and my mom presses her face to the window for a better look.

Tears roll down her cheeks. My grandma loses her composure and fumbles for words.

"Oh, Eleanor ... I'm so sorry," she cries.

"It looks the same as I remember," Mom whispers.

My grandma parks as close to the house as she can so that we can get Mom in easier. I shake Ellie to wake her up.

"We're here!" I say brightly, and Ellie gives me a sleepy smile. She grabs her teddy bear and steps out of the car.

Grandma and I each grab an elbow to lift Mom from the car. Her eyes remain fixated on the house. I can tell she's eager to go inside. We help her up the steps to the porch. Grandma unlocks the front door.

"I thought it'd be best for you to sleep in the bedroom on the main floor," my grandma says. "The stairs would be too much."

Mom nods.

"Mommy, your real room is upstairs!" Ellie tells her. We laugh because Ellie knows it was Mom's room when she was young, and, clearly, she thinks it's the better choice.

"I want to see it," Mom says. My grandma and I exchange a look. Those stairs will tire her out completely. As if she is reading our minds, she says, "I can make it. Just walk with me." I know we're not going to change her mind.

The climb takes a long time. Mom coughs and struggles for breath with each step. My grandma and I are practically lifting her small frame up to the next step to make it easier on her. We pause for several minutes about halfway up.

"Mom, are you sure this is a good idea?" I say. "Maybe we could bring your things downstairs for you to see instead?"

Mom shoots me a dirty look, and my grandma and I both smile. She's determined. I'll give her that.

When we get to the top, Mom swings open the door to her old bedroom. We stand back and watch her take it all in. She steps in and runs her hand along the posters on the wall, her flowery bedspread, and the photos on her corkboard. She fingers the jewellery on her desk. She stands staring at her drawings and the view from the window for what feels like ages.

"I left things the same," my grandma whispers. Her body trembles with guilt and sorrow. I rub her back, but my eyes don't leave Mom.

She turns to us. I expect to see her upset and sad but instead she is smiling wide.

"It's okay," she says to her mom. "I'm glad you left it like this. It's good to be home."

The two of them embrace. I sense the heaviness of my grandma's heart easing with my mom's forgiveness.

"Can I have some time alone in here?" Mom asks.

Neither of us wants to leave Mom alone. We step out of the room and close the door behind us, but we stay put outside the door. I shuffle my feet back and forth and stare at the marks I'm making in the plush carpet. My grandma fiddles with the rings on her hand and stares absent-mindedly at the ceiling while we wait.

When Mom opens the door, she grabs for our hands and we stabilize her and make our way back down the stairs. I see that she's been crying, but she seems content.

"Since I'm not the seventeen-year-old anymore, I guess that's your new room, Jayce," she manages. I smile and caress her arm.

"Okay, Mom. I'll take it."

Mom sleeps the rest of the day and night, so I'm especially relieved to see her sitting in a rocking chair on the front porch the next morning. Her oxygen tank is propped up beside her, and a thick patchwork quilt is draped over her despite the soaring June temperatures. Ellie and I have our bathing suits on and we run through the sprinkler together. I hold her hand and we count down before each leap into the spray of water. The water is freezing, and it shocks our pale bodies.

Grandma passes by with a basket of freshly picked flowers, and I think of Kurt and wonder how he's doing. I grab a bath towel from the clothesline. It is warm from the sun and it feels heavenly against my chilled skin.

"You are beautiful, Jayce," my mom says to me. She's been watching us intently. I blush and brush her comment off, but, secretly, it makes my heart leap.

"She is, isn't she?" my grandma agrees. "That's quite the young lady you've raised, Eleanor. You've done a terrific job."

One glance at my mom tells me that this remark from her mother makes her heart leap as well.

Mom sleeps for the rest of the day, but she wakes up at midnight. My grandma and I are still up. Neither one of us had been able to sleep, so we had decided to play a game of Scrabble. We both jump up in alarm when we hear Mom stirring in her room.

"Relax," she admonishes us. "I'm fine."

"Just stay there, Mom. We can get you whatever you need."

"I want to go out and see the stars," Mom says firmly. We help her to her feet.

When we swing open the door to the porch, it is pitch-black outside. The only sounds are the crickets chirping in the warm summer air. The sky is clear and brilliantly lit with stars. They are bright sparkles against the inky sky. The three of us sit in silence on the porch, gazing up at the sky in wonder. I'm taken aback by how small I feel, looking at this incredible sky. I think of what lies beyond — what other galaxies exist. Is there life out there?

Mom closes her eyes and points her face toward the stars, letting the soft breeze brush her cheeks. She is drinking in this moment. I wonder if Mom is wondering the very same things.

Chapter 25

We've only been in Meadow Lake for a couple of days, and already I miss Kurt. Despite Mom's illness overshadowing our days, we've had a wonderful time together. Mom seems happier, and Ellie and I are thrilled to be able to spend so much time with her. Grandma has been doting on all of us.

"Why don't you invite Kurt out here?" Grandma asks me while we're eating lunch.

"Really?" I ask. "That would be okay with you?"

"I miss him myself!" my grandma says. We all laugh. I look at my mom and she nods her approval. I excuse myself and start dialing Kurt's number.

That afternoon, I help my grandma with yardwork. I pull weeds and water the garden. She even shows me how to drive the riding lawn mower, which is really fun. I mow the entire lot myself. By the end I'm dripping with sweat from the intense summer sun, and I wonder how my grandma has managed all of this herself for so long. She keeps watching me with a big smile. I can tell that, even though she's grateful for the help, she's happy to have us here, period.

"Iced tea break!" my grandma calls. Ellie and I come running. The once-frosty glass is dripping wet from the heat of the day. It feels cool and welcoming against my sweaty palms. I gulp my iced tea in seconds, and Grandma pours me another one.

We are flipping through old photo albums on the front porch when Kurt drives up. Ellie runs toward him, and he gathers her in his arms and swings her around. Even my grandma rushes toward him and hugs him. She pulls him up to the porch and welcomes him in. He goes to my mom first and gingerly hugs her before coming to me.

"You okay?" he whispers in my ear when we hug.

"I'm good," I say. I mean it. Despite the challenges we are facing, there is a lot of love and laughter helping us through.

"I should probably grab my things," Kurt says.

"How long are you staying?" I ask him.

"Only a couple of days. You guys need your time together. I don't want to take away from that."

"I've made up a room for you, Kurt," my grandma says. "It's upstairs on the left. Jayce can show you."

I lead Kurt to the room he'll be staying in, and he sets down his bag and pillow.

"You have to check this place out," I tell him. He follows me back downstairs and out the door, and we walk around the lot. "It's gorgeous here."

"It's good to see you, Jayce."

"You, too, Kurt. I've been worried about you." We're strolling along the perimeter of the lot along the spruce trees. "How are you managing?"

"You know, sometimes I used to feel resentful about my situation. Caring for my grandma was a lot of work. I just wanted to be like any other teenager. But now that she's gone, I'd do anything to have her back. She was an awesome lady, and I loved her so much."

"Kurt, no one could fault you for that. How many teenagers are also full-time caregivers to their relatives? It wasn't a typical situation."

"No, it wasn't. But I see how lucky I was now. A lot of people don't get someone like my grandma in their life."

Kurt sees the swing and bounds toward it. "I gotta try this out!" I laugh as he climbs on the swing and starts pumping his legs. I think of all of the laughter and healing that's taken place at this homestead in the past few weeks. There's something about this place.

The next day, we all take a drive. It's squishy with the three of us kids in the back of the car, but we listen intently as Mom and Grandma point out landmarks around town. We see where Mom went to school and the places where she and her friends liked to hang out. I wonder if I'll be attending the same school in the fall.

"We could drive to the provincial park," my grandma offers, but Mom shakes her head.

"I don't think I'm up for that today," she admits. "Let's do that another day."

We stop at the KFC drive-through and pick up lunch. Although she will probably only eat a bite or two if we are lucky, the chicken is Mom's request. I balance the bucket of chicken on my thighs while Kurt holds the tray of drinks. As we drive down the dirt road to my grandma's house, we see a black sedan parked in front. I suck in my breath. I know exactly who it is, and my grandma does, too. She purposely parks away from the other car and points us facing the trees.

"Stay here," she says firmly. Mom's head is resting against the headrest. She has her eyes closed and doesn't even notice that we're parked away from the house. Ellie is having thumb wars with Kurt. He looks at me quizzically, but I don't say anything. I watch as my grandma marches over to the tall figure. He is standing beside the car and looking up at the house. He has seen us pull up, and when I catch a glimpse of his face I see how nervous he looks.

I can't hear their words, but I can tell from my grandma's body language that she is telling him to go. She keeps looking back at our car and it dawns on me that she is hoping my mom doesn't see him.

My grandma opens his car door for him and motions for him to get back inside, but he doesn't. His eyes squint toward my grandma's car, and then his face changes to one of resolve. He brushes past my grandma and makes his way toward us.

"No!" I hear my grandma yell. She runs after him and pulls on his arm, but he shakes her off and continues toward us.

"Oh, no," I whisper. Kurt's head whips around, and he sees the man heading toward us and my grandma trailing after him, panicked.

"Who is that?! What should I do?!" There is urgency in his voice. He knows something is wrong.

"It's okay," I say calmly. I've tried to protect my mom from him, but I know that there's no stopping what's about to happen now. "It's my dad."

Chapter 26

He does not look into the back seat for us. Instead, he opens the passenger's side door. My mom's eyes fly open in surprise, and she gasps when she sees him standing over her. He looks broken, his handsome face weary and sad. Even his salt-and-pepper hair looks drab and unruly. He reaches for her hand, but she pulls it away and keeps it from him.

"Eleanor," he says. His voice is strained and sad. His eyes are pleading with her to acknowledge him. She remains still and silent. I don't know what to do.

"Mom?" I say slowly. Ellie's eyes are wide at the sight of my dad here. All of ours are. How did he know where we were? Why did he come?

"Joe, you have to go," my grandma says. But I see Mom's face, and I know the damage has already been done. Our efforts to protect her from seeing him have been dashed.

"Eleanor," he says again, and this time his voice breaks.

I open the back door, and the three of us climb out of the car. My dad looks pitiful, standing there and hoping to talk with my mom. It's the first time they've seen each other in over four years, and I hope he sees every inch of pain on my mom's face.

Mom tries to get herself out of the car, but can't. My dad reaches for her, but she bristles and motions for Kurt. Kurt slides his arms behind her back and under her legs and carries her out in one easy motion. She looks so small and frail in his arms. It makes me sad to see how easy it is for Kurt to carry her. My grandma takes the oxygen tank and follows close behind as we all head toward the house, my dad last in tow.

"Get her inside," my grandma says, fumbling for her house key.

Kurt disappears with her beyond the front door, and Ellie runs in after them, leaving me and my grandma with my dad.

"Please," my dad pleads. "I need to talk to her. Just give me five minutes."

"This is not a good idea, Joe," Grandma says. "I think it would be best if you left."

"I need to talk to her," he repeats.

She remains steadfast and shakes her head.

"You didn't even tell me you were leaving Saskatoon. Were you trying to hide them from me? Did you think I wasn't going to find them? Of course I'd remember this place. I was the one who came all those years ago and picked Eleanor up when you threw her out, remember?"

My grandma bristles at his remark.

"I want to be part of my daughters' lives. They've lost too much," Dad says.

"That's fair," Grandma says. "But right now —"

Kurt appears in the doorway. "Jayce," he says. "Your mom wants to talk to him."

Before I can say or do anything, my dad marches straight through the door. My grandma and I both bolt after him, but Mom puts her hand up and motions for the two of us to go. We stare at each other, incredulous. It doesn't feel right to leave the two of them alone together. Neither of us moves. Mom waves at us again.

Grandma and I back out of the room reluctantly. Mom seems to be struggling more with her breath, and I want to berate my dad for stressing her out and putting her through this. We take Ellie by the hand and shut the door behind us, defeated.

"Sorry," Kurt says, as though somehow this is his fault.

"You did nothing wrong," my grandma tells him. "I just hope Eleanor knows what she's doing." We all stand nervously on the front porch, unsure of what to do with ourselves.

"Well, let's eat," my grandma says. None of us seems interested now.

We wait for what feels like an eternity. My ears practically burn with curiosity about what they are talking about. I wonder if he's trying to convince her of his love for her despite his decision to abandon us and marry someone else. How could he possibly explain away the hurt he's caused us? I wonder if he's begging her to let him have custody of us. I think about going to Prince Albert and having Mallory as my stepmom. She seemed like a nice woman, but I have no desire to live with her. I pray that Mom does not give him this option.

When my dad emerges from the house, he looks spent. "Your mom wants to talk to you," he says to me. I glance at him in surprise and run into the house. Mom is sitting in the recliner. She looks so strong and sure of herself sitting there.

"What did he want?" I demand.

"Jayce, it's fine," she replies.

"No, it's not. Was he trying to convince you of his love for you? How did he explain away how he left you to be a single parent and lied to you for years?"

"It wasn't that easy."

"Oh, sure. One bat of his eyes, and you fall all over again."

"Jayce!" Mom barks at me. The sharpness of her voice causes me to jump.

"Sorry," I say immediately.

"I believe your dad did love us. I really do. Did he make mistakes? Yes. Huge ones that he can't take back. Is he sorry and does he regret it? Yes, I believe he does."

"So you've forgiven him? Just like that?"

"Jayce, you're a magnificent daughter. You have helped so much. You've been practically another mother to your sister. She is so lucky to have you."

"Don't change the subject." I stare down at my hands. Tears start to drop onto my lap.

"I practically grew up with you; I was so young when you were born. And growing up means doing things like forgiving people."

"No. It sounds like it means you're giving up."

"I wish I could stay with you, Jayce. I don't know how much time I have left on this earth. And I need to know that you'll be taken care of."

"So, what? You're going to give us to him? You can't leave me with these people. You're the only stable thing in my life. You and Ellie. What if Grandma decides she's had enough of us, too?"

"You'll be fine. These people love you. They will be there for you." My mom holds her arm out for me to come closer and I kneel beside her and rest my head on her.

"But what if they're not?" I am hysterical now. How can she be so sure?

"They will, J.J. They made mistakes and want to make good on them now. And everyone makes mistakes and deserves another chance. Just give him a chance, Jayce."

"Your love is the one thing I've always been sure of," I sob into her.

"That will never ever change. No matter what happens to me, I'll always be with you," Mom assures me. She hugs me fiercely and kisses my head. I cling to her and cry until there's nothing left.

"How is she?" Grandma asks when I step back outside. She is clearly worried.

"She's okay. She's asleep again."

"Are you okay?"

"Yes. I'm fine." I'm surprised to see that my dad's car is still there, and I'm even more surprised when I see him pushing Ellie on the swing. "Is he staying?"

"No," my grandma says. "Not unless you want him to."

I shake my head no.

When my dad sees me back outside, he stops the swing and takes Ellie's hand and leads her back to the house.

"So, we'll be in touch?" I tell him, signalling him to go. I will not close the door on us. Although Ellie and I may have been robbed of a dad up until this point, we have the chance for one now. I know I don't want to go live with him, but that doesn't mean I can't still have him in my life in some capacity. Maybe we'll grow to have a good relationship. Someday.

"Okay, Jayce." He nods. It's not the answer he wants to hear, but he seems relieved that I'm open to working on things between us.

"My door is always open to you," he says. "I mean it."

I nod and bid him goodbye. He waves to everyone and then walks back to his car. We watch him pull away.

"I want to stay here," I announce, once Dad's car is out of sight. Everyone is watching me. It takes courage to say it but I say it again, "I want to stay right here. For good."

My grandma bursts into a smile. "Are you sure?" she asks. Kurt comes and puts his arm around me for support.

I nod. "If you'll have us." Tears cascade down my cheeks. Grandma rushes to me and pulls me so tight I can barely breathe. She motions for Ellie to come and join in and the three of us stand united.

"I've never wanted anything more."

Chapter 27

The next day, Mom rises for a bit in the morning and then goes back to sleep for several hours. When she wakes up, she is struggling for breath more than usual and doesn't have the energy to rise. We take turns sitting with her while she lies in bed. I braid her hair and read to her. She doesn't join us for supper that night.

"We've probably pushed her too hard the past couple of days," I say. Between the sightseeing and the encounter with my dad, we've sapped a lot of what little energy she has.

"Well, something tells me your mom wouldn't have had it any other way," my grandma says. She's right. Mom is determined to do what she wants to for as long as she can. We slurp the homemade soup that's steaming in our bowls and mop up the remains with freshly baked bread. I hope that Mom will eat when she wakes. The meal is heavenly.

"So, Kurt, I was thinking …" My grandma is rinsing her empty bowl. "There's really no sense in you driving back tomorrow. If you've got nothing pressing to get back to, why don't you stay?"

"I don't want to impose, Mrs. Nichols," Kurt replies. "I'll just make it a quick visit."

"Impose? You are part of our family," she says matter-of-factly.

"Thanks, but I really should go back and give you guys your time."

"You're not getting what I'm saying, young man." My grandma looks at him pointedly. "Why don't you think about coming to live here?" I choke on the last of my food. Live here? She's inviting Kurt to move in? His eyes are practically bulging out of his head in surprise.

"I'm a lonely old woman. I've wanted to fill this house up for years and years. Now I've got the three most important girls in my life here … how about we add you, too?"

Kurt looks at me to see my reaction. I smile and give him a little shrug of indifference, and then I break into a wide grin.

"Jayce, this is crazy …" he says to me.

"If I were you, I wouldn't mess with my grandma," I remind him. "You know she's a tough woman."

"I guess it's settled, then," she says smiling. "We'll get the details worked out, but I think it's a fabulous idea." She wipes the counter with a dishcloth and continues cleaning without another word. Ellie looks to me for confirmation and sees my smile.

"So does this mean you're my big brother now?" she asks innocently. Kurt melts when he hears this and gives her a sheepish grin.

"Sure, Ellie, I guess it does."

That night, my grandma joins me on the front porch under the stars. It's the middle of the night and everyone else has been sleeping for hours.

"How did you know I was out here?" I ask her, as she takes the seat beside me and drapes a quilt over our legs.

"I couldn't sleep, either."

We both gaze up at the night sky. "I'm sorry I was so horrible to you," I tell her.

"Jayce, we've already discussed this."

"I know, but I feel really bad."

"Are you sure about your decision?" she asks.

I belong with my mother, while she suffers from this disease that is battering her relentlessly. I belong with my grandma, who has been given a second chance with her family, and who has proven that she's sticking around. And that she loves us.

"Yes. Are you sure about yours?"

"I want you here more than anything."

The sky is so clear that I can see the Milky Way, along with a lot of constellations that I wish I could name. Mom would love this sky right now.

"It's going to be hard to lose her," I say.

Although we haven't been talking about my mom,

her illness and what it's doing to her is never far from our minds. My grandma nods.

"We'll help each other through it," she says, and I believe her. She wraps her arm around me and I lean into her shoulder.

I belong here in this house I've grown to love, where I'm surrounded by constant reminders of my mom. Everywhere I look, I can see snippets of her hopes and dreams for herself before she was thrust into parenthood. I knew so little about this time in her life before I came to Meadow Lake. Now, I've come to understand my mom so much better. We've also been able to heal and grow as a family here, in this humble piece of paradise. Our time together here has reminded me of what's important in life: family, friends, forgiveness, love.

I belong here, with my grandma, staring at the sky. I may not know what tomorrow will bring, but I can be certain that today I'm right where I need to be.

I'm home.

Acknowledgements

I can't thank Arnold Gosewich and Dundurn Press enough for making this book possible. Thank you to Kirk Howard, Carrie Gleason, Shannon Whibbs, Karen McMullin, Cheryl Hawley, and the rest of the team at Dundurn Press — working with you has been a wonderful experience both times around. Shannon, your gentle guidance made this story stronger and richer. Thank you!

Publication and edits of this book came together during a scary, challenging time in my life. I found myself ill for several weeks, in and out of the emergency room, and bedridden with heart trouble. My husband became my full-time caregiver, and life as I knew it took a really long and frightening pause. I send a heartfelt thank-you to Deidre Craig, Carla Shoforost, Sabrina Tabler, Chantal Banda, Megan Peter, Jill Blom, Kami Hnatiuk, Gerri Perrault, Erik Olson, Aimee Mainil, Earl and Amie Kowalczyk, Janice Cook, Bev Theriault,

Jim Sharman, and Doug and Molly Scarrow, as well as countless other friends from our children's school community — without your generous hearts and assistance during this time, I'm not sure we would have made it through. Please know that I will go to the ends of the earth for each of you. This experience has allowed me the good fortune of discovering a village I didn't even know I had. I want to be part of your village, too.

I would like to thank my reading group: Maria Deutscher, Susan McMillan, Leandra Clarke, and Bev Theriault. Your feedback and advice is invaluable to me.

Thank you to my mom, Bev Theriault, for being such a great sounding board and source of support. Once again, you powered through each draft with me.

Nothing is possible or worth anything without the love of my family. To my Scarrow, Theriault, and Deutscher families, I love you and thank you for your continued support.

To Ben, Gracelyn, Ethan, and Kale, thank you for the gift of time to write and for allowing me to do this all over again. It really is a thrill beyond measure.

By the Same Author

Throwaway Girl
Kristine Scarrow

**When your teen years are so messed up,
how do you grow up happy?**

Andy Burton knows a thing or two about survival. Since she was removed from her mother's home and placed in foster care when she was nine, she's had to deal with abuse, hunger, and homelessness. But now that she's eighteen, she's about to leave Haywood House, the group home for girls where she's lived for the past four years, and the closest thing to a real home she's ever known.

Will Andy be able to carve out a better life for herself and find the happiness she is searching for?

Of Related Interest

Since You've Been Gone
Mary Jennifer Payne

Fifteen-year-old Edie Fraser searches for her mother, who has gone missing shortly after the two moved to London, England, to escape Edie's abusive father.

Is it possible to outrun your past? Fifteen-year-old Edie Fraser and her mother, Sydney, have been trying to do just that for five years. Now, things have gone from bad to worse. Not only has Edie had to move to another new school — she's in a different country.

Sydney promises her that this is their chance at a fresh start, and Edie does her best to adjust to life in London, England, despite being targeted by the school bully. But when Sydney goes out to work the night shift and doesn't come home, Edie is terrified that the past has finally caught up with them.

Alone in a strange country, Edie is afraid to call the police for fear that she'll be sent back to her abusive father. Determined to find her mother but with no idea where to start, she must now face the most difficult decision of her life.

In Search of Sam
Kristin Butcher

When Dani sets out to uncover her father's past, she also discovers her own future.

Raised by her mother, eighteen-year-old Dani Lancaster only had six weeks to get to know her father, Sam, before he lost his battle with cancer. It was long enough to love him, but not long enough to get to know him — especially since Sam didn't even know himself.

Left on the doorstep of an elderly couple when he was just days old and raised in a series of foster homes, Sam had no idea who his parents were or why they had abandoned him. Dani is determined to find out. With nothing more than an address book, an old letter, and a half-heart pendant to guide her, she sets out on a solo road trip that takes her deep into the foothills, to a long-forgotten town teeming with secrets and hopefully answers.